'I found a bottle of white in your fridge. I hope that's all right?'

Charlotte turned around to hand him a glass and took a sip from her own. Hunter watched the liquid coat her lips and a sudden thirst came upon him which had nothing to do with alcohol.

'Was tonight so bad that you couldn't wait for me to get back?' he teased, and took a drink before placing the glass back on the kitchen counter.

'I thought it would get the wine and music out of the way quicker so I could see what else you had planned.' She bit the inside of her cheek as she teased him right back.

He slowly and silently took the glass from her and set it down. Somewhere in the distance the saxophone sounds of nineties power ballads set the mood for seduction as he moved in. 'Nothing's planned. I thought we'd just see where the night takes us again.'

It took him straight to her parted lips, to indulge in the tangy taste of wine and temptation. He inhaled the scent of her sweet perfume as he bunched her hair in his hands and deepened the kiss. She was most definitely real—and his for as long as she wanted.

Over these past days she'd given him everything he could ever have asked for: joining forces to help him in work and at home, and trusting him not to let her down. That was a big deal, given her past history, and he wanted more than anything to prove he was worth the risk.

Dear Reader,

'Ice Hockey Dude', as my hero Hunter has been affectionately known throughout the writing process, has been in the planning for a very long time. Ice hockey is a relatively new sport to Belfast, and—as in the town in my book—it brought much excitement with it. Along with a host of handsome Canadian players who did indeed fall in love with local girls and are still here over a decade later. A romance novel just waiting to happen!

As with all bad boys, Hunter Torrance has taken some taming, but with the help of my fabulous editor, Laura, I've finally wrestled him into submission. Now all we need is Charlotte Michaels, the team doctor, to forgive him his sins too and learn to trust him again…

Happy reading!

Karin xx

REFORMING
THE PLAYBOY

BY
KARIN BAINE

Published in Great Britain 2017
By Mills & Boon, an imprint of HarperCollins*Publishers*
1 London Bridge Street, London, SE1 9GF

© 2017 Karin Baine

ISBN: 978-0-263-06938-9

Printed and bound in Great Britain
by CPI Antony Rowe, Chippenham, Wiltshire

Karin Baine lives in Northern Ireland with her husband, two sons, and her out-of-control notebook collection. Her mother and her grandmother's vast collection of books inspired her love of reading and her dream of becoming a Mills & Boon author. Now she can tell people she has a *proper* job! You can follow Karin on Twitter, @karinbaine1, or visit her website for the latest news—karinbaine.com.

Books by Karin Baine

Mills & Boon Medical Romance

Paddington Children's Hospital

Falling for the Foster Mum

French Fling to Forever
A Kiss to Change Her Life
The Doctor's Forbidden Fling
The Courage to Love Her Army Doc

Visit the Author Profile page
at millsandboon.co.uk for more titles.

This book is for my sisters, Heather and Jemma,
who first got me hooked on ice hockey and encouraged
my stalking of No. 28! Also for Jaime and Lucy,
the next generation of Giants fans.

Thanks must go to Andrew, because without his help
I never would've been able to write this book. Or so he
would tell you. And to Ricky so he doesn't feel left out!

It's been a rough few years for all of us and,
though I never say it, I love you all. xx

Finally, to fellow author Annie O'Neil.
You've been an angel, and although we've yet to meet
you've become such a lovely friend.

Listen to the rhythm

CHAPTER ONE

IF ALIENS HAD landed in the middle of this rural Northern Irish town and declared her their new supreme leader, Charlotte Michaels couldn't have been any more surprised than she was now.

'Hunter Torrance? *The* Hunter Torrance is the new team physiotherapist?'

Although he was standing there, casting a shadow over her, she didn't quite believe it. Didn't want to believe it. The Ballydolan Demons was *her* team, *her* responsibility, and having ice hockey's most infamous bad boy on board wasn't going to dig them out of the hole they were in.

'Yes. Deal with it, Charlie.' We need him.' Gray Sinclair, the head coach, delivered the news and strode away, leaving her face-to-face with the new signing in the arena corridor. She'd been on her way to watch the team train when the pair had ambushed her and literally stopped her in her tracks.

'Hunter Torrance, the new physio. For now. I guess my future employment will be dependent on results.' The latest addition to the team held out his hand as he introduced himself but she wasn't inclined to shake it until someone convinced her this wasn't some sort of sick joke.

'Like everything around here,' she muttered. He wasn't the only one on trial. This was her first season as team doctor, and so far, with the list of injuries they had, a run of poor results and the last physiotherapist quitting on short notice, it could be her last too.

With a build more like a willow tree than the mighty oaks usually associated with the sport, she'd worked hard to be taken seriously but now they'd landed her with a side-kick who still held the UK Ice Hockey League record for most time spent in the sin bin she was worried the professionalism of the medical staff would be in jeopardy. The ex-Demons player had undermined the team's position in the league once before and she wouldn't sit back and let him do it again. In any capacity.

He smiled at her then, even as she ignored his offer of friendship. It was a slow, lazy grin, revealing the boyish dimples which had made him a pin-up for many a girl around here. Her included. If someone had told her at eighteen she'd be working alongside this one-time NHL hunk some day she would've died with happiness. Now the sight of him here was liable to make her forget she was a strong, independent career woman and not that same vulnerable teen. Something she had no time for nine years on.

He hadn't changed much in that time, at least not physically. Although this was probably the closest she'd ever been to him without the Perspex partition separating the players from the fans. He was still as handsome as ever, only now the pretty boy-band looks had morphed into the age-appropriate man-band version. Those green eyes still sparkled beneath long, sooty lashes, his dark hair was thick and wavy, if longer than she remembered, and he was dressed in a black wool coat, tailored blue shirt and jeans rather than the familiar black and red Demons kit. Damn but he'd aged well; the mature look suited him. It was a shame she could barely look at him without the abject humiliation of her past feelings for him spoiling the view.

'It's good to be back,' he said, and continued walking towards the rink as though he was returning to an idyllic childhood home and not the scene of his past misdemeanours.

For a moment Charlotte contemplated walking back in the other direction and locking herself in a nice quiet room somewhere until he'd gone away. He'd appeared from the shadows as if he were a bad dream. Or a good one, depending on which Charlotte was having the fantasy—the young infatuated girl or the cynical woman who knew bad boys weren't exciting or glamorous, they just screwed people over.

She didn't. Instead, she followed him towards the ice. Hunter wasn't to know she'd been enamoured with him to the point of obsession the last time he'd been on Northern Irish soil but he had cost her beloved Demons the championship with his antics. Even if she hadn't been embarrassed by her teen fantasies she still wasn't convinced he was up to the job and simply didn't trust him to do it effectively.

'Why are you here?' Her forthright attitude obviously wasn't something he was used to, or expecting. She could see him tensing next to her and she didn't like it. To her, the guarded reaction meant he had something to hide. The very nature of his defensive body language said he was fighting to keep his secrets contained but she wouldn't be fobbed off easily when it came to work matters.

'No offence but you're an *ex*-player for a reason. The drinking, the fighting, the generally bad attitude...they're not qualities I look for in a co-worker either.' His last appearance here had been a coup for the Demons to have him on board when no other team would have him. A big name for a budget price. Unfortunately, even this easygoing community hadn't been enough to tame his wild ways. He'd become a liability in the end, his playing time down to single figures for his last matches, as opposed to the many minutes he'd spent in the penalty box. Eventually people had given up on him. Charlotte too, once she'd realised he wasn't the man she'd thought he was when he'd snatched success away from the team. There'd been a collective sigh of relief when he'd flown back to Canada and she couldn't say she was happy to work alongside someone prone to such unpredictability now either.

'Ah, so you witnessed that particular phase of my life? In which case I can't expect you to be performing cartwheels on my return but I can assure you I'm here to work, not to raise hell.' Something dark flitted across his features that said he was deadly serious about being here, and sent chilly fingers reaching out to grab Charlotte by the back of the neck. She wanted desperately to believe that having him here would benefit the team, not hinder it, but she needed more proof than his word.

'I don't understand. Why would you want to come back to a team that holds memories of what I imagine was a very dark time for you? Especially to work off the ice rather than on it?' She made no apology for her blunt line of questioning. It didn't make sense to her and she'd made it a rule a long time ago to question anything she deemed suspect. She'd learned to follow her gut feeling rather than blindly take people at face value. It prevented a lot of pain and time-wasting further down the road.

'Despite…everything, I like the place. I want to make this my home again. There's also the matter of laying a few personal demons to rest and proving to you, and everyone else, I'm not that same hothead I was nine years ago.' It had taken Hunter some time to answer her but when he did he held eye contact so she was inclined to believe what he was saying, even though she doubted it was the whole truth.

'I trust you have all the relevant qualifications and experience?' Although she expected his appointment was more to do with his connections here and last-minute availability than actually being the best man for the job, she couldn't stop herself from asking. She needed someone who knew what he was doing on the medical staff with her.

'All my papers are in order if you'd like to see them.' He was teasing her now, the slight curve of his mouth telling her he wasn't intimidated by her interrogation technique.

'That won't be necessary,' she said, folding her arms across her chest as a defence against the dimples. This so wasn't fair.

'Look, I'm the first one to admit I was a screw-up. Not everyone will be happy to see me back but I'm sure we're all different people now compared to who we were back then.' He leaned back against the barrier, his coat falling open for a full-length view of the apparently new and improved Hunter.

That giddy, infatuated fan who shared Charlotte's DNA insisted on taking a good, long look. Who was to say that Mr Sophistication here wouldn't someday regress back to his rebellious alter ego too?

She'd never been a fan of that particular side of him. The young girl she'd been then had enjoyed the macho displays of the defenceman body-checking his opponents into the hoardings or dropping his gloves in a challenge fight. There was something primitive in watching that, even now, and there'd been times she'd wanted someone to defend her the way he had his teammates. He'd definitely been a crowd- and a Charlotte-pleaser for a time. But those later months when he'd fought with his own coach and smashed equipment in bad temper had made for uncomfortable viewing. It had felt like watching someone unravel in public and had come as no surprise to anyone when the Demons, or any team, had refused to renew his contract. He'd slunk back to Canada in disgrace, never to be heard of again. Until today.

'Clearly Gray thinks you've changed since this was his doing and he's the man in charge, not me. Well, I mean, if I was in charge I'd be a woman, not a man...'

'Obviously.' Hunter dropped his gaze to her feet and she followed it all the way back up to her eyes. He may as well have had X-ray vision the way he'd studied her form so carefully, smiling whilst she burned everywhere his eyes had lit upon her.

No, no, no, no, no! This wouldn't do at all. Behind the scenes of an ice-hockey team was not an appropriate place to suddenly become self-aware and he certainly wasn't an appropriate male to be the cause of it. These men were out of bounds. All of them.

Hunter mightn't be a player, or one of her patients, but he was a colleague. Given their past history, albeit a one-sided affair, his presence here complicated matters even more for her. With the team languishing in the bottom half of the league her position was already a tad precarious, without him in the picture too. Especially when he kept looking at her as though he was trying to pick her up in a seedy bar.

'Well, I'm sure you'll want to meet the team...' She backed away, reminding herself this wasn't about her, Hunter or any ridiculous crush. They were both here to do a job and a team of sweaty, macho hockey players should be a good distraction from any residual teenage nonsense.

'Maybe later. I wouldn't want to disrupt training. We should probably use the time to get to know each other better so I can convince you I'm not here as some sort of punishment.'

'That's really not necessary.' Charlotte gave a shudder. She knew all she needed to know about Hunter Torrance.

Probably more than most due to her teenage obsession and enough for her to want to keep a little distance between them.

'Hey, we're both on the same team, right?'

'Not by choice,' she muttered under her breath.

It was no wonder the powers that be had kept this snippet of information from her until it was too late to do anything about it. She'd been surprised they'd found a replacement physiotherapist willing to see out the last few games of the season and hadn't asked any questions, simply glad to have help getting the team back to fighting strength for the play-off qualifiers. Now she knew the good news had come with a catch.

'Well, I'll do my best not to get in your way. Actually, I wasn't even expecting you to be here today. I thought team doctors practically only made appearances on match days with the slew of outside commitments and specialist clinics you all usually have to boost your salaries. I know this is a different league from the NHL in terms of rules, technical terms, profile and especially finances. Or are you the official welcome committee?'

She knew he was deliberately being facetious as he took a little payback for the hard time she'd given him so far. His sneer earned him her narrow-eyed stare, which usually had the power to wither a man at fifty paces, but the bad boy of the tabloids took it all in his stride. What was a dirty look in the grand scheme of things when she supposed his whole past would probably be raked over again in the national press when they got wind of his return?

'Clearly, I didn't get the memo we'd have a VIP joining us otherwise I would have dusted off my pom-poms.'

Hunter opened his mouth to say something then seemed to think better of it and simply shook his head. It was probably a good idea. She wasn't in the mood for innuendo-based banter in the workplace, even if she had left the door wide open for it.

'In answer to your question, I'm here for the play-off matches. I schedule my sports and musculoskeletal clinics around my time here so I don't miss anything.' It wasn't easy but she used her personal leave to make sure she was here for the most important dates on the hockey calendar.

'I'm sure there aren't many who have such commitment.' He seemed impressed that she took her role here seriously but that only made her blood boil a fraction more. If he'd ever been as dedicated as she was to the game he would understand the sacrifices she made. Experience had taught her Hunter wasn't the team player the Demons needed.

'This is my team. I want to see them win and I'll do what I can to help realise that dream, but we do have our work cut out for us at the minute. Carter has a meniscus tear, Jensen has bursitis, Dempsey a groin strain, and Anderson, our star player, needs a serious attitude adjustment.' She listed those battling injury who were already causing concern for the upcoming matches. He needed to understand the workload was substantial and this job wasn't simply a position with a title.

'I'm sure we can manage between us. After all, that's what I'm here for. Not to make your life more difficult or to cause trouble. Those days are long gone. What do you say we start over with a clean slate and work together to get this team back on its feet?' He held out his hand in truce, asking that she forgive whatever sins he might've committed in her eyes.

Perhaps she was overstepping the mark here when she wasn't in any position of authority but she'd thought someone should have the Demons' best interests at heart when Gray's judgement seemed clouded by sentiment, or sympathy, or something that had no business in his team decisions. Still, the deed was done now and as a professional she knew better than to let her personal feelings get in the way of doing her job.

'Fine.' She hesitantly reached out towards him and shook on the new partnership. Her hand tingled where Hunter's gripped it so confidently and it wasn't simply because of the sheer size and power of him, making her fingers seem doll-like compared to his. There was also the moment of fantasy and reality colliding in that touch. Hunter Torrance was *actually* in her life now.

She inhaled the fresh, citrus scent of his aftershave so deeply she made herself dizzy. An entirely primal reaction that probably would've happened whether she'd known who he was or not.

For most single women he'd be the perfect package. If tall, dark, handsome and Canadian did it for you. Which it did. Why else would she be sniffing him as if he were made of chocolate and she wanted a taste? He was wrong for her on so many levels so she'd simply have to resist licking his face.

She'd done her best to fit in here as one of the crew, and making doe eyes at the new recruit wasn't very professional, it was asking for trouble. And it had definitely found her in the shape of a six-foot-four, two-hundred-pound ex-hockey-player.

Okay, so she still had stats memorised, it didn't mean anything other than she'd once been a girl with way too much time on her hands. An unhappy girl from a suddenly broken home who'd sat in her room like some fairy-tale princess in a tower, waiting for her knight in shining armour to come and rescue her. Except her hockey-playing knight had turned out to be an immature mess who had stolen the chance of that championship title from her beloved Demons and fuelled the theory all men had the ability to inflict mortal wounds to the heart. Not so much galloping off into the sunset as a life sentence distrusting anyone who dared come too close.

She knew her hostility towards him would seem un-called for, petty even. That didn't stop her from hoping his past might catch up with him and send him back to the land of snow and ice. He'd shown he wasn't a man to be relied on when his team needed him. Surely she wouldn't be the only one to hold a grudge?

In his short time here he'd insulted and fought with many, had damaged the reputation of the club and gener-ally been a pain in the backside to all those around him. Not everyone would be glad to see him return and she was kind of hoping those with a legitimate reason to give him a hard time would, to save her blushes and her posi-tion on staff.

Gray, the coward, had apparently left it to her to break the news to the others. It had taken all of her inner strength *not* to protest, *You were on that team he decimated, you should know better than anyone why I think he's a liability.*

She hadn't because she did her best to keep her passion for the game and her job separate. There was no fair rea-son he shouldn't be here if he had all the relevant experi-ence needed for this job.

'Guys? Can we have a quick word?'

The team trooped off the ice and lined up, waiting for the news. Charlotte swallowed hard. There was definitely no going back now.

'We just wanted to tell you there's a new addition to the medical staff. Hunter Torrance will be your new physio-therapist for the rest of the season.' She didn't sugar-coat it. They could come to their own conclusions about what this meant. Her only job had been to relay the message and she'd done that as quickly and as bluntly as she could so this was over soon and she could go home to lick her wounds.

'What?'

'*The* Hunter Torrance?'

'You're kidding!'

There was a stand-off moment as they stood looking blankly at each other, no one knowing what to do with that information, including Hunter. He was frozen beside her, probably trying to decide on the fight-or-flight method of defence. She knew which one she'd prefer and would happily book him a one-way ticket back to Canada.

The first stick hit the ground with a heavy thud, then another, and another, until he'd received a round of applause hockey-style.

Floret, the captain, stepped forward and shook Hunter's hand first. 'Good to have you on board.'

Charlotte figured the move was because he was a fellow countryman but he was soon followed by the rest of the multinational squad.

'You're a legend, man.'

'Dude, I'm sure you have stories to tell.'

Charlotte rolled her eyes as they surrounded their new physio as if he was some sort of rock star. The last thing she needed was the players taking their cue from him that bad behaviour would ultimately be rewarded.

At least Hunter had the good grace to look slightly embarrassed by the positive attention. In her opinion he didn't deserve it and by the way his cheeks had reddened and he was trying to back away from the crowd she guessed he didn't think so either. Too bad. They were both stuck in this hell now.

'They're all yours,' she muttered as she walked away unnoticed and left him at the mercy of his adoring fan club.

After all, he'd insisted he could handle them and she was done for the afternoon. With the play-off matches looming, which could see them knocked out of the Final Four Weekend in Nottingham, they'd soon find out if the ex-rebel had turned over that new leaf and could justify his new place with the team.

The fan in her wanted him to work some magic and help get them match fit to fight their rivals for that place in the finals but she was a cynic at heart. She'd rather not take the chance of getting her hopes up, only to be disappointed at the last moment.

Hunter hadn't come to ruffle any more feathers. He had enough old enemies without making new ones and he certainly hadn't intended on upsetting the resident doctor. Gray had called in too many favours for him, none of which he deserved, to screw this up now. His old teammate was the one person who knew what he'd been through and had been willing to give him a chance. One he was grabbing with both hands.

Those selfish, heady days were far behind him now. There was only one reason he was back in this County Antrim town and that was for his son.

Hunter Torrance, the responsible father. It was the punchline to a very sick joke. A disgraced hockey player who'd barely been able to take care of himself now found he was the sole parent to an eight-year-old boy who'd just lost his mother in a car crash. He'd only had a few months to get used to the idea of being a father and to grieve for the relationship he could have had with Sara, the ex-girlfriend who'd hid the huge secret from him. Perhaps if he'd been in the right head space back then, able to love her, they could've been the family he'd always dreamed of having.

Instead, he'd walked away from her, consumed by his own self-pity, and returned to Edmonton.

For as unreliable as the old Hunter had been, the new one was as determined for his son to have the stable up-bringing he'd never had. So he'd given up everything he'd worked hard to rebuild back home to do it. Now all he had to do was convince Sara's parents, Alfie's grandparents, and everyone else here he was up to the job.

He'd expected an initial backlash over his appointment here from the players and fans but not from the rest of the medical staff. This doctor probably knew nothing of him beyond his reputation yet it seemed enough to warrant her displeasure at the prospect of having to work along-side him. Not that he could blame her. The back-slapping welcome he'd received had come as a surprise to him too. Tales of his hockey days were probably a novelty to young, up-and-coming players still caught up in the thrill of the game.

For those who'd been personally affected by his behav-iour, himself included, he'd prefer to confine his exploits to the past, and he'd told them so. After he'd confirmed or denied several of the urban legends attributed to his name and number.

'Is it true you spent longer in the penalty box than on the rink for the last month of your career?'

'Yes.' He wasn't proud of it. He hadn't been trying to play the villain or even defend his own players. The issues from his childhood that he'd tried to suppress had finally come to the surface in an explosion of misdirected rage. Years of therapy had taught him that but it wasn't infor-mation he was willing to share, or a time of his life he was keen to revisit. He was a different man now. Hopefully one more at peace with his past and himself.

'Did you really punch a linesman and knock out his teeth?'

Hunter sighed. He'd long since apologised to the unfortunate man whose offside decision he'd so violently opposed. 'One tooth, but I'm afraid to say I did.'

He didn't want any impressionable young talent to think his past behaviour was an advertisement for anything other than career suicide. 'It cost me my place on the team, my life here, everything.'

By that stage he'd been completely out of control, drinking too much, lashing out and acting out the role of a child in pain seeking the attention of a family that didn't want him. Ironically it was that behaviour that had made Sara turn her back on him and deny him a chance of a family of his own.

'I imagine tales of my debauchery have been greatly exaggerated in my absence. It's probably best you don't believe everything you've heard about me and form your own opinion. Which mightn't be any more favourable when you see the new programme I've devised for you...'

Whilst a new, intensive regime wouldn't endear him to his new buddies, it was his way of proving he was serious about his job here. He hadn't moved halfway across the world to be one of the guys; he was here to make a difference to the team and secure a future for him and Alfie. Gray had clued him in on the challenges he was up against and it was possibly the reason he'd secured the job against the odds—no one else was willing to take on the responsibility of a struggling team at such short notice. Hunter had done his homework and he knew exactly what he was up against but he'd been training for this ever since he'd hit rock bottom and had decided he wanted his life back in whatever capacity was available to him. After years of therapy and retraining he certainly wasn't going to be put off by the thought of some hard graft.

If only Charlotte had stuck around she would've seen the adoration had been short-lived. He'd come prepared with notes and ideas on strengthening and stability exercises for the guys. As a player he knew how much stress the joints and muscles went through. The mechanics of the game and the repetitive actions left the body vulnerable to injury and even a slight strain could easily become a nagging injury, refusing to heal. It was his job to prevent more serious problems further down the line as well as treat them. Regardless of her departure, he'd forged ahead in implementing his new exercise regime, strapped up those who'd needed a bit of extra muscle support and massaged any problem areas in preparation for these next important games.

He'd gone on to treat Colton's groin strain with a myofascial release of the muscles involved, manipulating the connective tissue with a sustained, gentle pressure to help regain function again.

Murray's torn meniscus, caused by the trauma of the knee joint being forcefully twisted, thankfully wasn't severe enough to warrant surgery. Hunter worked to strengthen the muscle surrounding the knee and add to the stability of the joint. The excess swelling and pain were treated with anti-inflammatory medication.

He was sorry Charlotte hadn't been here to witness his switch back into business mode. His commitment should make her job a little easier too. After all, the medical team was supposed to work together to get the most from the players. It wasn't an in-house competition to decide who deserved their place here over the other.

The noise of the crowd and the smell of the crisp, clean ice took Hunter back to his own game nights, and gave him the same adrenaline rush it always had. His first match tonight wasn't so much about that final score for him but about his personal performance. He wanted to make a good impression and shoot down all the naysayers who still believed he was a liability in any capacity here.

He filed down the players' tunnel with the rest of the game crew. It was odd being part of the team without being *part* of the team. He was almost anonymous, standing here in the shadows. The way he preferred it. It was circumstance that had dragged him back into the outer edges of the spotlight.

He ventured out far enough to glance around the arena, trying to pick out those present who'd brought this sudden and dramatic change to his way of life.

'Are you looking for someone?' Charlotte appeared beside him.

'Er...no one in particular.' The seats he'd arranged for Alfie and his grandparents were still empty but he wasn't going to share that information with anyone. He'd learned the hard way to keep details of his personal life out of the public domain and he wasn't about to jeopardise his chances of getting custody of his son for anybody. Even if it might take that look of disgust off her face.

The intense reaction he was able to draw from her with minimal goading fascinated him and he didn't know why, beyond wondering what he'd done to deserve it. She wasn't his usual type, at least not the old Hunter who'd enjoyed the company of more...appearance-obsessed ladies who'd revelled in their sexuality. Sara hadn't been bold or brash but she'd certainly given her feminine attributes a boost with beauty treatments and figure-hugging outfits.

Charlotte was a natural beauty, shining brightly through her attempts to disguise it. Even wearing her game crew red fleece and with her chestnut-brown hair swept to one side in a messy braid, she was as pretty as a picture. He wouldn't deny it but neither would he act on it even if she didn't treat him as if he was the devil incarnate. They were co-workers and all women were off limits for the foresee-able future. For once he had to think about someone other than himself and Alfie's well-being came before hockey or his love life.

'Well, if you can drag yourself away from whatever has caught your interest, the game is being played in *that* di-rection.' She nodded towards the ice, obviously mistaking his keenness to see his son for something more lascivious.

Given his reputation, it wasn't a huge stretch of the imagination that she should jump to that conclusion but he did wonder if she would ever give him the benefit of the doubt when it came to questioning his commitment to the job. Especially since he had no intention of correcting her or making her aware of Alfie's existence. They weren't close enough for him to share such personal information and as first impressions went he didn't think they were going to be best buds any time soon.

Still, he did take a certain pleasure in her *tut* and the roll of her eyes before she stomped away in temper. It was good that she took her work seriously but she really needed to loosen up. He wasn't the enemy, even if it was fun play-ing the part now and again.

Hunter's smile died on his lips as he wrenched his gaze away from his colleague's denim-clad derriere and back to the crowd. Sara's parents were in their seats, watching him with disapproval etched across their faces. Whilst he'd been busy with Charlotte he'd missed their arrival and had fallen at the first hurdle by ignoring his son in favour of a woman. It had taken a while simply to get them to tell Alfie he was his father and this was the first time he'd been allowed to see him outside their home.

They didn't want Alfie's parentage to be public knowl-edge any more than he did until things were settled a bit more. Their caution was understandable when he'd already left their daughter in the lurch and probably ruined her life. Unfortunately he couldn't do anything to make amends for their loss but he could try to be the parent Alfie needed him to be.

He gave a wave, his eyes now only for his son, and the swell of love that rose in his chest for the excited little boy waving back put everything into perspective once more. It didn't matter what anyone else thought of him as long as his son loved him, trusted him enough to be with him.

The O'Reillys weren't against the idea of him having custody as long as it was in the best interests of their grandson. All he had to do was make sure he was match fit for the parenting game and leave the old Hunter back on the ice. Along with any wayward thoughts towards his fiery new colleague.

CHAPTER TWO

THE ATMOSPHERE AROUND the arena was electric, everyone buoyed up for the game against the Coleraine Cobras and the chance of getting one step closer to the play-off finals. The Demons were the underdogs at present and to secure their place they needed to come out on top after playing one home and one away match to the Cobras, who were sitting at the top of the league table. It was a tall order but Charlotte kept faith along with all the other fans.

She could hardly believe she was now part of the action instead of a mere spectator sitting in the stands with everyone else. It was a privilege to be on the ground floor of the establishment but she'd also worked damned hard to get here. There was no way she would let everything she'd achieved slip through her fingers for the sake of one man's ego. Whatever, or whoever, had brought him back to town needed to take a back seat for the team's sake.

She'd had to swallow her pride and come out to stand alongside Hunter in the tunnel because that's where she needed to be—on site and focused on the players. It didn't stop her unobtrusively watching him as the lights dimmed and the crowd was whipped into a frenzy with roving spotlights and blaring sirens hailing the arrival of the home team.

Each time the lights fell on his face for a split second

she could see his eyes trained on the ice waiting, watching for that puck to drop. As intense as he'd always been.

A shiver danced its way along her spine as she recalled those past games when she'd found it difficult to watch anything other than him on the ice. It wouldn't do to regress to that sort of infatuation again and for once she should follow his example and get her head in the game. Although he perhaps wasn't as single-minded about tonight as he'd led her to believe. She'd caught sight of him waving to someone in the crowd. Someone who'd made him smile. Not that she was jealous. She pitied him really that he couldn't be alone in his own company for five minutes without the need to hook up with a woman.

The single life suited her and she believed she was stronger without a partner to fret over. Between her and the apparently lovestruck Hunter she knew she'd be the one giving her all to the team without distractions. Not everyone would put the Demons first in their life the way she did, but it was concerning he had other priorities already. They didn't need any more drama behind the scenes and if he really was serious about being part of the squad he ought to be focusing somewhere other than the contents of his trousers. It gave credence to the notion he was only back here for Hunter Torrance's benefit, not the Demons'. She doubted he'd be willing to put in the overtime or go the extra mile the way she did if he had other pursuits outside working hours.

The first two periods of play were relatively uneventful, with both sides playing it safe and focusing on defence, so there were high hopes and expectations for the third period. Especially when the Demons had several near misses, with more attempts on goal than their opponents.

'Come on, guys.' Hunter's booming voice and the thump of his hands clapping as he willed the Demons to score didn't make it easy for Charlotte to concentrate on what was going on inside the rink instead of the decoration around it.

'You must miss this.' She hadn't meant to say it aloud when they'd seen the rest of the game out in virtual silence but he was so involved, animated on behalf of the team, it occurred to her how hard it probably was to no longer be part of the action. He'd skated on this very ice, played for this very team, and seen out the last days of his career here. She'd only been a fan so her position was akin to a lottery win in some aspects while his could be seen as a demotion, standing on the sidelines now.

The roar of outrage from around the arena after a high stick incident against one of their players drowned out her observation.

'What's that?' Hunter didn't take his eyes off the play but leaned down so he could hear her better.

She swallowed. This wasn't supposed to be a *thing*, it was simply her mouth opening before she'd realised. Now he was standing so close to her she could almost feel the rasp of his stubble against her cheek.

'I...er...was just saying you must miss this.' It sounded so feeble the second time around it really wasn't worth repeating.

Of course he missed it. Hockey had been his career, his life at one time. It had been a stupid thing to say, right up there with the people who asked her if she missed her mother. Duh. Generally not unless someone brought her up and made Charlotte realise how incomplete her life was without her in it. Now she'd done the same thing to him.

'Sorry. I should be following the game too, not chatting.'

For the first time since face-off he focused his full attention on her, his eyes bright and his smile wide. Enough to make her stop breathing.

'I do miss it. However, as has been pointed out to me, I'm probably more of a hindrance than an asset to the team these days.' His mischief-making brought the heat to her cheeks, and everywhere else.

To all intents and purposes he was the team's new signing, doing his best to fit in, and she'd acted the superior know-it-all, making life difficult for him. She didn't know this man yet she'd made preconceived judgements and behaved accordingly when he'd been nothing but friendly in the face of her childishness. For someone who was all about equal rights in the workplace she knew she wouldn't have been so forgiving if a colleague had been so awful to her for no apparent reason. A little teasing in return wasn't something she should complain about.

For a second she thought about apologising. The truth was, he *was* an asset. He'd treated all those on the injury list the way any experienced physiotherapist would have. She'd checked. It was her, letting her personal embarrassment over an old crush get in the way of a harmonious working relationship.

In the end she kept her mouth shut because she didn't trust herself not to blab about her past devotion for him when she was looking into those eyes that had once stared at her from her bedroom wall. Worse, she might go the other way and insult him again so he didn't realise she was having inappropriate thoughts about him.

She had to block him out of her sight and focus back on the game, something she'd never had any trouble doing before. Usually it was more a case of not losing herself in the match and making sure she was watching the players for signs of injury. Sometimes separating Dr Michaels from fan-girl Charlie took a great deal of effort.

The dizzying pace of the players covering the ice was as heart-pumping as it got for her. The hard-hitting alpha males and the danger of the sport had always been like catnip to a girl whose life had become so troubled and lonely. That was probably why she'd been instantly drawn to Hunter the first time she'd attended a game. Everything about him had said danger and excitement.

It still did.

The hairs prickled on the back of her neck and she knew Hunter was close again before he even spoke.

'Is there something wrong with Anderson I should know about?'

The object of his concern was already on her radar, a bit more sluggish than usual, which was worrying when he was their star player.

'He has missed a few training sessions lately, which would account for him being more breathless than usual. His fitness needs working on. I'll put a word in with Gray, if he hasn't already picked up on it himself.' She doubted she'd have to point anything out. Anderson was popping up on everyone's radar lately with his diva attitude. As top goal scorer they'd let his stroppy behaviour slide but now it was affecting his performance someone was going to have to take him to task.

'Hmm. It looks more serious than that to me.'

Anderson had been making rookie mistakes all night, getting caught offside and hooking the opposition with his stick in full view of the ref.

'I assure you he'll get a full physical after the game and if I find any areas for referral I will let you know.' This was her jurisdiction and it didn't matter who the new physio was, she was still the medical lead.

They watched Anderson shoulder-charge everyone out of his path. With the giant chip perched there these days it wasn't difficult to do.

'And if the problem's mental, not physical?' Hunter

crossed his arms, his shirt tightening and vacuum-packing his biceps in white cotton.

'Well, it would also be down to me to make that judgement call.'

Not you. Back off.

He smirked and shook his head. Charlotte tried to ignore it but he was so far under her skin he'd burrowed right into her bones.

'What?' she finally snapped, the thought of her past infatuation sneering at her too much to take.

'I get it. You're the sheriff in this here town and I'm merely your deputy.' He tipped his imaginary Stetson and she conceded a small smile. Well, it was better than swooning after that image and a Southern drawl double whammy.

'And don't you forget it.'

They locked eyes for a second too long, the laughter giving way to something more...serious. She looked away first and let the background game noise fill in the gaps in conversation. Just when it seemed as if they were starting to bond, stupid chemistry, or stupid rejuvenated teenage hormones, tried to turn it into something she didn't want, or need, in her life.

Before she was tempted to take another peek at him, a face was mashed into the Perspex in front of her, the violent thud shaking the very ground beneath her feet. The distorted features of a Cobra player slid down the glass, making her wince. She was always conflicted when it came to such territorial displays of male aggression. As a fan, it was a barbaric form of entertainment, watching your team dominate the other. As a medical professional, she understood the physical ramifications of such an impact and as the on-site doctor she'd be called on to treat any injuries caused to the opposition too. That was why she was standing here with her first-aid bag by her feet, for those players who couldn't shake it off and get back on their feet.

The shrill peep of the ref's whistle pierced the air.

'What was that for?' Charlotte demanded to know, along with most of the crowd rising from their seats as Anderson was reprimanded.

Hunter flinched. 'He checked him from behind. That's gonna cost him time in the penalty box.'

'Oh. I didn't see that,' she said, cowed by her own mistake. She knew it was an illegal move because it carried a risk of serious injury but she couldn't tell him she'd missed it because she'd been busy gawping at him.

'I'm guessing he hoped everyone else had missed it too. Now what's he doing? He messed up. He should own it and do the time.' Hunter threw his hands up in despair as Anderson remonstrated with virtually everyone in authority as he made his way to the penalty box.

His gestures imitated that of a clearly frustrated Gray too as he yelled at his star player from the bench. The coach was a disturbing shade of purple as he fought to control his temper and she made a mental note to check his blood pressure.

Anderson's penalty left the Demons short-handed for the dying minutes of the game and Charlotte held her breath with every other fan desperate to keep the dream alive. There were so many bodies in the goal crease as they fought for a victory it was difficult to make out who had possession. Until the klaxon sounded and the red light behind the net flashed, signalling a goal.

The Demons had defied the odds and claimed a win, sending the crowd into a furore, but Anderson's mood didn't improve when the game was over and he left the ice. He stripped off his kit and threw it piece by piece down the tunnel in temper as he clunked past Hunter and

Charlotte, unleashing a string of expletives directed at no one in particular.

Despite his public celebration with the team on the ice after their narrow win, Gray's demeanour changed too when he approached them. 'I don't know what the hell is wrong with Anderson but he needs sorting out before the next game. You two are supposed to be the experts around here. Find out what's eating him and fix it, or don't expect to be signing new contracts any time soon.'

'Gray—' Hunter tried to put a hand on his shoulder in an apparent attempt to calm him down but he shrugged it off.

'I pulled a lot of strings to get you here, Hunter, and I expect a lot in return. I don't care if you talk to him as an ex-pro, sports physician or a fellow maniac, it's your job to get him match fit and right now he's following in your footsteps to career suicide.'

She could almost hear Hunter's heart fall into his shiny shoes with a thud as his so-called ally cut him down with a few cruel words. The hand of friendship fell slowly to his side, the pain of rejection chiselled into his furrowed forehead. Her previous disparaging comments aside, she kind of felt sorry for him. His past misdemeanours were always going to be thrown back in his face regardless of his subsequent achievements and acts of repentance.

'There's really no need for that, Gray.' She put herself in Hunter's position for the first time and thought how it might feel to have someone cast up the naivety of her youth. Horrendous. Soul-destroying. Unfair.

She'd spent a lifetime distancing herself from that person and if he was to be believed, so had Hunter. Switching careers from hockey pro to qualified sports therapist wasn't something that would've happened on a whim. It would've taken years of dedication and determination. All of which was being cast aside as if it was nothing because someone was in a bad mood. Or because someone was deflecting the shame of their own past.

Gray held his hand up to stop her. 'It goes for you too, Charlie. Fair or not, I need results. I'm sure you can come up with a diagnosis and treatment plan between the two of you. After all, that's what you're here for.' With that, he spun on his heel and powered towards the changing room.

She lifted an abandoned puck from the ground and tossed it in her hand, tempted to lob it in his general direction. Two could let temper get the better of them.

Hunter caught it in mid-air. 'You don't want to do anything you might live to regret, Charlotte.' That serious face said he was speaking from painful experience. One he'd never be allowed to forget.

She let her aggression subside with a sigh, partly due to his voice of reason and perhaps because he'd used her name for the first time. Everyone here called her Charlie, in keeping with her efforts to remain one of the guys. Her full name, in that accent, made her feel positively girly. Even in her game night layers of fleece and comfort.

'He'd no right to say any of those things. At least, not the personal stuff. I guess he's kind of right about the reason we're here. He just didn't have to be so rude about it,' she huffed on his behalf, since he seemed determined not to rise to it. Not so long ago she imagined he wouldn't have thought twice about charging down there after him and duking it out.

Perhaps he had changed. Perhaps he did deserve to have someone give him the benefit of the doubt. Then again, if his one friend here couldn't let go of the past and fully trust him, why should she?

Hunter shrugged, those broad shoulders refusing to carry any more baggage upon them. 'He's right. He did call in a lot of favours for me. I owe him big time.' Either he had really matured or he was putting on an award-winning performance to dupe her into thinking he had. Especially when she was the one chomping at the bit to retaliate.

She had to remind herself he didn't owe her anything personally; there was nothing to be gained in convincing her he was anyone but himself, except to prove his commitment to the job.

'So what do we do?' Stitches and concussion she could deal with. A burly hockey player with his finger on the self-destruct button was out of her comfort zone.

'I wouldn't want to step on your toes…' He held up his hands in mock surrender to her self-appointed superiority.

'Okay, okay. If I have to tackle an irate man twice my size, I could use the backup.'

And because Gray had said so.

'We can't do anything until we've seen to everyone else. We're going to have our work cut out for us back there, after that last scrum especially.'

'Then what? The chances Anderson is waiting patiently back there for counselling, treatment or another rollicking are slim to none.'

They had no clue what was ailing him and from her experience thus far, hockey players were stubborn about admitting any weakness. There was definitely more of an 'I can tough it out' attitude to injury than she was used to from other athletes. It made her job that much more difficult when those niggling pains turned into something more serious left untreated.

If it was some sort of chronic or traumatic acute injury sometimes it could mean the end of a career. In which case, Anderson would be even less inclined to admit there was a problem. Male pride could be a terrible affliction if left unchecked.

'You heard Gray. *We* have to find him.'

She let out her breath in a huff, which may or may not have had to do with his continual glances into the crowd.

'Unless the Demons have taken to tracking their players, how on earth are we going to do that?' By the time they finished up here he could be anywhere. It would be dark, and she would be more than a bit cheesed off with the whole drama. Especially when she was expected to do it with Mr Torrance and that brought him much too close for comfort.

'If I know my hockey players, and the heart of any Northern Irish town, there's only one place Anderson will be sitting his time out. Let's hit the pub.'

If she didn't love her job so much she would've left him to it but these were still her players, her patients, her team, and she wasn't afraid of dropping the gloves herself to fight. It wasn't only the Demons' honour at stake here.

Not only was Gray frothing at the mouth despite the result but Hunter was struggling to find those feel-good endorphins too. It was his son's first match, the first time he'd seen his father's team in action, if not playing himself, and he hadn't been able to share it with him.

'Sorry I couldn't sit with you tonight, bud.' He managed to catch Alfie and his grandparents before they disappeared out of the arena and into the night.

'That's okay. Maybe we can come again?' He glanced up at his guardians with the same hope Hunter was still clinging to.

'We're coming to the end of the season now but perhaps I could bring Alfie for a tour behind the scenes some time?' It was a big ask, he knew, but if he was to win over his son he had to start fighting for time alone with him.

Alfie's face lit up but his grandmother shut down the notion of any unauthorised trips with a stern 'We'll see'.

The light began to dim again before flaring back to life. 'Maybe Dad could come back with us for supper?'

It was the first time Alfie had called him Dad and it choked Hunter up that he was even starting to think of him in that role. It killed him to have to let him down.

'It's getting late and I still have some work to do here. Another night, bud.' He knelt down and Alfie rushed towards him, hugged him so tightly it brought tears to his eyes. He didn't care he could barely breathe because he'd never been as happy as he was in this second. This was the beginning of the family he'd never had and the pieces were finally slotting into place.

'Come on, Alfie. It's bedtime.'

Although Hunter was thankful for the opportunities afforded him to get to know his son, he was looking forward to the days when there wouldn't be a time limit set on their relationship.

He slowly and reluctantly peeled Alfie from around his neck. 'I'll see you again soon. You be good.'

The kiss he dropped on his son's head inadequately expressed the love he felt for this child he'd been without for too long but it was all he had to give for now.

Someday they'd be watching the games and eating popcorn together before going home to their own house. Until then they'd have to snatch whatever time was granted by those who thought they knew what was best.

''Night, Dad.'

''Night, son.' He waved the trio off, watching them safely across the road until he was too misty-eyed to make them out.

He sucked in a deep breath of the cool night air to fortify his aching heart and blinked away his sentimentality. It was time to focus on the positives. Alfie was happy and safe and he had a job to do. He'd prefer to keep it that way.

It was close to midnight before they were able to leave the arena. His, or Anderson's, personal problems had to wait until the players who actually hung around after the game were properly cooled down. Ice baths and stretches were equally as important as the warm-up to keep the muscles in prime condition. He knew Charlotte had a few nicks and grazes to treat on both teams but nothing serious or unusual for men in close contact with sharp blades every day of the week. He came to knock on her door just as she was lecturing her last patient.

'Remember: RICE. Rest, ice, compression—'

'And elevation. I got it, Doc,' a weary Evenshaw replied as she strapped up his ankle.

Hunter gave him a hand down off the bed and watched him limp away. 'I hope that's nothing serious.'

'A slight sprain,' she said as she packed away the dressings and other bits and bobs she'd used to patch players together again.

Now she'd ditched her zip-up outer layer he could see she was wearing a white round-neck T-shirt. It wasn't a particularly remarkable piece of clothing, forgettable, if it wasn't for the fact she'd unwittingly exposed her toned midriff as she'd yawned and stretched.

He coughed away the sudden surge of awareness heading south of the border. It had been a long time since he'd had the pleasure of seeing a female body who wasn't a patient, otherwise he wouldn't be responding like a virgin seeing a naked woman for the first time.

'I hope you're not too tired to go Anderson-hunting?'

Although it might be better if she was. Regardless of Gray's insistence and the prospect this could somehow improve working relations between him and Charlotte, he was beginning to have doubts this was a good idea.

He kept losing focus when he was around her, not concentrating on the game or the arrival of his VIPs but watching spots of colour rise in her cheeks as he baited her. There'd also been that moment when she'd stood up for him against Gray. That had been unexpected. From both sides.

Clearly he and his one and only friend still had unresolved issues. Although Hunter knew Gray had said those things in the heat of the moment, there was truth behind them. He'd let him down in the past and though the words had hurt, he'd deserved them and Gray had needed to say them. He just hoped now he'd got it off his chest they could move on again. He wouldn't dwell on it when he knew how much more pain could be caused by letting a grudge fester out of control. It had already ended one career and he didn't think he had it in him to start over again if this didn't work out.

No, it was Charlotte's attitude that had been most surprising when she'd been the most outspoken about his reputation so far. Perhaps they were starting to make progress after all and she was no longer seeing him as the Ballydolan Demon come to life. Whatever it was, it had felt good to have someone on his side after all this time. Someone whose opinion of him appeared to be turning and she wasn't afraid of saying it out loud.

'Of course I'm not too tired,' she snapped.

'Of course you're not,' he replied. For a woman who appeared so delicate on the outside she wasn't afraid of much. He got the impression she'd trawl the whole of Ireland even if she was dead on her feet if it meant sticking two fingers up at the doubters.

'Where do we start?' Charlotte was back at his side, refusing to let him forget her.

'Wherever's within walking distance.' He set off at a brisk pace, determined to get this over with and get back to his bachelor pad as soon as possible. Minus company.

'How do you know he hasn't just gone home or taken a six pack off into the woods?' Charlotte was almost running to catch up with him as she struggled back into that hideous jacket but he didn't slow down for her. With any luck she'd get fed up and go home.

That was as likely as Anderson being tucked up in bed.

'I know we Canadians are a hardy lot but we're not stupid. That would mean having to go into the bar to buy booze and take it away. Dark woods might appeal to a brooding romantic hero but he's a hockey player, he needs to blow off steam fast.'

'He could have gone home like any other disgruntled employee after a hard day at work,' she grumbled under her breath, but she didn't know hockey players the way he did.

It was much easier to understand Anderson's state of mind when you'd been there yourself. If he was anything close to following the same pattern he himself had, not only would he be somewhere, getting drunk quickly, he'd be spoiling for a fight to unleash some more of that aggression they'd witnessed earlier.

'It's possible but if we're thinking logically, there are about six bars on the route back towards his house.' He'd asked around for details, not that there were many forthcoming. Although he knew where Anderson resided there was little information about his personal life. It wasn't because the players were reluctant to share with him—in that respect they seemed quite open to him, probably because of his hockey background. No, it seemed no one knew much about Anderson outside the team or alcohol-fuelled nights out. That in itself was dangerous. Hunter understood only too well how isolating it could be out here with no family around to catch you when you fell and pull you up by the scruff of the neck. Perhaps if he'd had someone do that for him he might've salvaged something of his sports career.

'I don't know why they need so many pubs in such a small space anyway,' she bristled, every inch the reluctant partygoer, and he was beginning to wonder why she was so against the idea of calling in at the local establishments when it was the obvious place to start their search.

Maybe she was teetotal, although that seemed as farfetched out here as leprechauns and their crock of gold.

'So you have somewhere to go when you get kicked out of the last one?' Well, that's how he'd treated the place when he'd done his fair share of drinking and brawling here. Strangely, it had only seemed to ingratiate him more with the locals. Until he'd taken it too far, of course, and cost them the championship.

There was a very unladylike grunt behind him but he refrained from continuing the argument. Anderson was close by, he'd put money on it. The sound of the *craic* coming from behind the doors and the draw of the liquor would be too much to resist.

They started their bar crawl at The Ballydolan Inn, the first dingy building no bigger than one of the nearby cottages at the bottom of the hill. Once they made their way past the smokers outside they were hit with a wall of noise as the doors swung open. The deafening roar soon died down to a curious silence as the locals eyed them suspiciously. If this had been a Western his trigger finger would be itching, waiting for someone to make their move.

Voices rumbled low but Hunter caught the mutterings about 'that hockey player'.

He scoured the interior, imagining an angry, drunk, Canadian forward would stand out in this crowd of regulars. When he saw nothing but curious Irish eyes staring back, he was ready to leave too. He wasn't up for another round of twenty questions about his personal life after leaving this place under a dark cloud and turned to chivvy his companion back out onto the street. 'Let's try the next one.'

They received much the same welcome there at The Hillside Tavern.

'Isn't that the big hockey fella who went nuts a few years back?'

'Aye.'

'Thought he'd be dead by now.'

'Used to play hockey. No longer *nuts*. Definitely not dead but very much older and wiser.'

Hunter tackled the rumours head on as they flew around him.

There was much more back-slapping after that, propelling them both towards the bar.

'Glad to hear it.'

'Sure you'll have a wee drink for old times' sake.'

It wasn't long before a space was cleared at the bar for them.

'Your local drinking establishment?' Charlotte mocked with a raised eyebrow, finding difficulty imagining him partying in here during his time with the Demons. In her head he'd been living it up in the clubs in Belfast or exclusive house parties for the rich and famous. If she'd known he was only down the street she might have socialised a bit more herself.

'Once upon a time. It hasn't changed much.'

'I doubt it's changed at all in the last century.' It still had the dark wood interior she remembered, permeated with the smell of the peat fire and sweat.

'I suppose we should really find out if there's more

than one hockey player they've been doling out booze to tonight.' She was beginning to see how easy it would be to fall into the drinking culture here. Honestly, there wasn't much else to do at night. When the game had first come here over a decade ago it had been a godsend to the young inhabitants like her, giving them somewhere fun and exciting to go without getting into trouble.

He shook hands with the landlord. 'Sorry, not tonight, Michael, I'm still on the clock. Have you seen one of ours in here? Anderson?'

'There was a big, blond fella who talks like you in here earlier but he was a bit worse for wear. He made a nuisance of himself, to be honest. Spilt a few drinks, broke a few glasses. I had to chuck him out. Sorry, if I'd known he was with you—'

'I'm sure he'll not be too far away. How long ago was this?'

'A good hour ago, I'd say.'

'Thanks.' Hunter grabbed her hand and bolted out the door with a renewed sense of urgency. The electric touch of his strong fingers clasping hers sent her pulse racing as they stole back out into the night.

He let go of her long after they had an excuse to be holding hands.

She absent-mindedly rubbed the palm of her hand where his had crossed it, mourning the loss of his touch already.

'Do you really think we're going to catch up with him?' She was a little on edge, spending so much time with Hunter. Every minute together altered her perception of the man she'd loved and hated in equal measure without ever knowing him beyond his public image. It was unsettling to find out he was as normal as anyone else. She'd moved past her crush a long time ago but she was worried it might take her somewhere more dangerous than a shallow physical attraction if she wasn't careful.

'Oh, aye.' His attempt at the local accent couldn't fail to make her laugh and she was rewarded with a toothy grin.

She'd always thought him attractive—that was a no-brainer. What teenage girl wouldn't have had her head turned by a handsome sportsman from a distant land? Finding out Hunter hadn't the hero she'd imagined him to be had been the biggest betrayal of all. Her mistake had been compounded by watching him fall apart before her eyes in those last matches until he'd convinced her there wasn't actually anything more than good looks and bad attitude there.

His short time back in the country was already beginning to change that opinion when he was doing whatever was asked for him to aid the team. That eye-opener spurred her on over the crest of the hill towards the old brick building with the faded green 'Kelly's' sign.

She was saved from further personal revelations as a rather large, unkempt figure came barrelling out of the pub door to land at their feet on the pavement. It didn't take a genius to work out what the cheer from inside and the sight of a burly barman dusting off his hands at the door meant.

'Anderson?' Hunter hunched down and brushed the dirty, bloody mop of hair out of the face of the unfortunate who'd been swiftly tossed from the premises.

'That's me,' he said with a slur. 'Gus Anderson. Man of the match. The crowd go wild.'

He was cheering now, swaying from side to side and pumping his fist in the air.

'Someone's got a high opinion of himself.' Charlotte was having second thoughts about helping if he really was this deluded. He'd almost cost them the match, the play-offs and their very jobs tonight.

'He's wasted. He doesn't know what he's saying.' Hunter struggled to get him onto his feet and although he didn't ask her to, Charlotte felt compelled to help.

She ducked under one arm of their patient, bolstering his left side. He weighed a ton, even though she knew Hunter was probably shouldering most of the weight.

'Er...now what? How are we supposed to fix *this*?'

'We can take him back to my place.' Hunter was already a bit breathless bench-pressing the man mountain so she hoped he lived somewhere close before all three of them ended up in a ditch by the side of the road.

They half dragged, half carried their wayward charge until they came to a cottage down the lane past Kelly's.

'This is your house?' The pretty chocolate-box cottage and garden didn't seem very *him*.

'Here, hold him until I get the door open.' He deposited most of Anderson's bulk around her shoulders and stopped her asking any of the questions flooding her head as she fought to stop her body being concertinaed into the ground.

Are you renting? Did you inherit? Does your girlfriend live here with you?

In hindsight she suspected that was the very reason he'd been so ungentlemanly in the first place. Whatever the secret, he wanted to keep it to himself. Thankfully, once he opened the door and found the light switch, he shared the burden with her until they were able to dump Anderson into a nearby chair.

'We'll need to get him cleaned and sobered up.' Gray would be expecting results and now under the glare of the living-room light she could see Anderson was a bit battered and bruised.

'Let's see if we can get him up to the bathroom.' Hunter steered them towards a narrow staircase and they somehow managed to manoeuvre him into the shower cubicle, still fully clothed.

A grinning Hunter switched on the water and closed the bathroom door on Anderson's shrieks as he underwent some sobering cold-water therapy. He backed out of the room, bumping into Charlotte in the cramped hallway. She stumbled back, tripping over the upturned edge of the faded hallway carpet. There was that helpless moment when she felt herself overbalance and tip over the edge of the staircase. All she could do was brace herself for the hard, painful landing she knew was coming.

Hunter shot out an arm around her waist, catching her before she fell off that top step and pulling her roughly against his chest, knocking the breath out of her.

'Sorry. I thought we should get out while he's cooling off. I didn't mean to nearly break your neck in the process.'

Her adrenaline was pumping as much from the near miss as being pressed against his hard body.

'You're forgiven.' She aimed for a friendly smile to hide the fact he'd unnerved her by being so close but her heart was pounding so hard she could no longer hear anything but the rush of blood in her ears.

For an instant their eyes locked, this intimate moment between the two of them frozen in time. His eyes darkened as they lit on her smiling lips and the conspiratorial joviality seemed to fade. He was watching her with such hunger, such focus there was no denying what it was he wanted, what he wanted to do to her. Just as before, she felt herself submit helplessly to gravity, only this time it was pulling her ever closer to his lips.

'Hey, you guys are too cruel. What, are you like SAS trainers or something?' Anderson yanked the door open and exploded the fantasy.

Hunter wrenched away from her so quickly he'd probably left friction burns in the carpet.

Charlotte was more appalled by her own behaviour. They'd almost kissed. Totally inappropriate with a work colleague, especially when there was every chance he was involved with someone else. So they hadn't actually made lip contact but she was pretty sure the intention had been there on both sides and that was bad news all around. Clearly she hadn't yet reached her lifetime's worth of humiliation where this man was concerned.

'I'll get some coffee on the go.' Hunter took the stairs two at a time in his obvious haste to get away.

She waited until she heard him banging about in the kitchen before she dared follow. At least Anderson, who'd ditched his sodden clothes for a bath towel, made for a distraction from the sudden atmosphere in the house.

She reached for her trusty first-aid bag, which she'd been carrying all night, predicting it would end in some sort of medical emergency, and pulled out an alcohol wipe to cleanse the deepest scratch on his face.

'Ouch!' He drew in a quick breath as if she'd poured salt into an open wound.

'Seriously?' She'd barely touched him and, with the stench of alcohol emanating through his very pores, she'd imagined he was probably numb from the scalp down.

'It stings, man.'

'Sorry. I'll be as gentle as I can.' Perhaps she'd been a tad more abrasive than she should have when she was angry at herself for the incident at the top of the stairs. She should know better than to let her personal feelings leak into her professional manner. Although Anderson was the reason she'd been thrown together with Hunter tonight, it wasn't his fault she'd thrown herself *at* him.

'What happened back there anyway?' She tried to turn

her thoughts back to her patient's current predicament, not her own, but it was easier said than done when she could still imagine Hunter's arms wrapped around her.

'At a rough guess I'd say a disagreement with some Cobra fans. Am I right? That's where the opposition hang out when they're in town.' Hunter handed him a mug of black coffee and offered her one without any indication this was in any way awkward for him after what had just occurred.

She declined. A nightcap of any description here wasn't going to happen. Once she had her big, brave soldier patched up she was packing up and running back to the safety of her own house, where she could analyse the reasons behind that almost-kiss.

Her patient took a sip of the strong-smelling brew and winced. 'Just some friendly rivalry.'

'Hmm. Well, it looks like one of your new friends took serious offence to something you either said or did. That cut on your cheek is going to need stitching.'

He was fortunate it wasn't closer to his eye but she'd lecture him tomorrow when he would remember it. It was too bad she wouldn't forget the events of tonight as easily because she knew they were going to change everything between her and Hunter at work. If she wasn't careful things were going to get even more complicated than they already were.

CHAPTER THREE

CHARLOTTE WENT TO wash up and proceeded to suture the deep cut. Hunter knew it was saving them all a hospital trip but the longer she spent in his house, the antsier he was becoming. They'd had one close call already. Only an irate Canadian water rat had pulled the brakes on that near-kiss that had come from nowhere and yet had seemed so natural. That was a direct contravention of his new dad regulations. He hadn't figured romance into his future plans at all.

As Charlotte tended to her patient, whose massive frame was wedged into the floral old-lady furniture, it struck Hunter how odd the set-up here must've appeared to her. At the time of renting the place he'd thought only of being close to Alfie. The owner had been keen to sell if he decided to stay permanently since this had been his late mother's house. One day Hunter imagined he and Alfie would put their own stamp on the décor. Until then he'd have to put up with the crocheted blankets and rocking chairs.

'All finished.' Charlotte had done a neat job, even in these unusual circumstances. Not that he was surprised when he'd seen and heard exactly how passionate she was about her work. The Demons were lucky to have her, yet Anderson hadn't even bothered to thank her.

He had an inkling they were all in for a very long night.

In the old days Hunter's first reaction to dealing with the stresses of the evening would've been to head straight to the bar. Whilst he was sorely tempted, it wouldn't solve any of their problems, so he served himself a shot of caffeine and took his position in the therapist chair.

'Do you want to talk about what happened tonight?' It would be easier than having him tear up the house in another rage-filled rampage.

Anderson eyed Charlotte sideways through his mop of wet, straggly blond hair.

'Surely you're not suddenly shy now? Charlotte's seen all of your antics tonight, don't forget.' Regardless of their personal faux pas, he didn't think she'd walk out if they were about to make a breakthrough here. As far as he'd seen, she always put her job first and wouldn't be sidelined when it came to the players' treatment on anyone's account.

'Anything you say in front of us is strictly confidential. We just want to help, Gus.' She took a seat next to Hunter on the couch, confirming that she wasn't going anywhere.

Anderson sighed. 'These Irish chicks…it's like they bewitch you or something.'

He was shaking his head but there was a ghost of a smile in there somewhere behind all that hair. It was a start, an opening to what was going on beyond the Hulkish façade. Hunter would've agreed except he didn't want his captivating companion beside him knowing that's exactly what she was doing to him. That was the only explanation of why he was veering so dangerously off track from common sense.

If there was one thing guaranteed to make a man want to smash stuff in a testosterone-fuelled rage it was woman trouble. Make that two things. Parents who wished you'd never been born had the same effect.

The big guy was on his feet, pacing. Hunter scanned the room for valuable antiques he should probably remove before he was charged for breakages but he was sure he could afford to lose the ugly owl ornament on the mantelpiece made from seashells and the tears of frightened children.

'This place was only supposed to be a stopgap, somewhere I could make a name for myself and move on.'

The opposite of Hunter's career slide into oblivion here. It had been the beginning of the end for him when he'd been shipped out here but a young, up-and-coming star like Anderson had a future in the UK league, maybe even the NHL, if he didn't screw it up too.

'Unless there's something you're not telling us, the only one putting that in jeopardy is you. Trust me, that temper is gonna get you attention for all the wrong reasons. Whatever you've got going on, deal with it now before your name is one no team wants attached to them.' It was true for him almost a decade later, even with a change of career. If it wasn't for Gray throwing him a lifeline he'd be stacking shelves in the local supermarket.

Gus flopped back into the chair and Hunter waited quietly so he didn't spook his unpredictable companion. Charlotte seemed to be of the same thinking as she remained quiet too. Neither of them would benefit from him kicking off again. Instead of forcing the issue, they let silence dominate.

He'd learned a lot from his own counselling sessions where the onus had been on him to fill the gaps in conversation. In the end the uncomfortable lack of interaction had forced him to verbalise the feelings he'd been avoiding since seeking out his birth family, and confront the crushing damage their rejection had caused to his self-esteem and self-worth.

It had taken him years to tackle the subject and understand he wasn't the one who'd done anything wrong. By which time it had been too late and he'd lost everything and everyone else. If he could prevent the same thing happening to his friend here, he would.

Whether there was a physical or emotional issue behind his behaviour, he needed to ask for help, instead of hiding behind the villain mask and pushing everyone away. He might've processed what had happened to him in his past, apportioned blame to the right people now and finally moved on, but that didn't mean there wasn't lingering frustration at having blown his hockey career along the way.

'Maggie's pregnant.' Anderson finally punctuated the silence with his shoulder-slumping admission.

Charlotte let out a long breath beside him. So it wasn't a serious injury he was battling but it was potentially a mess. At least he was opening up. It was progress; the first step towards salvaging the man and the player.

'And Maggie is?' Hunter wasn't assuming anything. She could be a fan, a one-night stand or a married woman for all the anguish this situation was apparently causing.

'We've been seeing each other for a few months. I mean, I like her. I really like her but I'm not ready for this.'

'Okay. This isn't the end of the world. I mean, I know it's a big shock but it happens to people every day and they live through it.' Charlotte attempted to reassure him and Hunter could almost see her mind ticking over, trying to figure out how they could help him come to terms with impending fatherhood.

He resisted a lecture on contraception when it wasn't going to make any difference now but he might suggest to Charlotte that they provide some literature on the subject to try and prevent more unwanted pregnancies or STDs among the players in the future. Although it did make him a feel a bit of a hypocrite when he'd made the same mistake at this guy's age. The only difference between him and Anderson was he hadn't known about Sara's pregnancy.

Perhaps that had been for the best. He hadn't been in the right frame of mind to be a father to Alfie then, or a supportive partner to Sara. By all accounts, they'd had a happier life without him and it had taken reaching rock bottom alone for him to finally get the help he'd needed to be the best dad he could be for Alfie.

'How does Maggie feel about it?' Of course it was Charlotte who remembered there was someone else's feelings in the equation here.

Gus looked at her as though it was the first time he'd even considered the effect it would have on his probably equally young girlfriend. The arrogance of youth.

'She's scared about how her parents are going to react to the news. I'm sure a hockey player wouldn't be their first choice for their daughter's baby daddy.'

'I hear ya.' Even without the drinking, fighting and generally acting like a jerk, he suspected Sara's parents would always have disapproved of him. Everyone, including him, had known he wasn't good enough. Sara and Alfie should have had a stable, reliable guy with a steady job to support them. He was doing his best to be that man for Alfie now. That's why the idea of getting together with anyone, even Charlotte, was dangerous.

He didn't miss Charlotte's raised eyebrows as he sympathised but he wasn't ready to share his own surprise baby story with anyone just yet. 'Do you have any family of your own here, Gus?'

He shook his head. 'We keep in touch from time to time but I haven't seen them for a while.'

It was too easy to distance yourself from family when living abroad, even if they did care about you, and they were the very people who could save a person from total despair. Unfortunately his hadn't.

'I would really make the effort to talk to your parents about this. You and Maggie both need the support. As someone who was effectively stranded here without any sort of emotional backup I would advise making the most of it so you don't end up making the catastrophic decisions I did.' So he'd shared a little personal info but it would be worth it to stop someone else making those same mistakes and throwing away the chance of a happy family.

Charlotte shifted in the seat next to him but he couldn't bear to look at her and see any hint of pity there. This wasn't supposed to be a group therapy session, he genuinely just wanted to help and the best way to do that was by showing some solidarity.

Anderson frowned. 'I really couldn't deal with their disappointment on top of everything else.'

'I know it's going to be a difficult conversation to have but, trust me, you don't want to go through this alone. Right now you're reacting on an emotional level. You need that grounding. Someone to give you a kick up the backside to start thinking clearly. If I'd had parents who'd given a damn, who I could've turned to for help when I needed it, I might never have left here in the first place.' Even now it was hard not to be bitter about the hand he'd been dealt: two sets of parents who'd happily sat back and watched him self-destruct. The only person who'd been there for him had been Sara but he'd been in too much pain to even let her get close emotionally.

'Hunter's right. This is too big to keep to yourself. If you're still on good terms with your mum and dad, swallow your pride and at least pick up the phone to talk to them if you can't visit in person. Make the most of having them in your life because you'll miss them when they're gone.' Charlotte was leaning forward in her seat, her arms wrapped around her waist, and he recognised that self-protecting gesture of someone who'd experienced that same isolation and loneliness, even if her experience of family sounded vastly different from his.

'You've both lost your parents?' The roles were reversed as Anderson took over the role of therapist.

'Mine aren't dead. They just wish I was. Neither my adoptive nor birth parents are in my life. Their choice, not mine.' There was no point dancing around the facts but it did make for an awkward silence as the blunt statement made an impact and he wondered if he had over-shared after all.

'I...er...did lose my mum a few years ago. My dad, much like Hunter's family, has decided he'd rather not be part of my life.'

Hunter wanted to lean over and give her a hug but she probably wouldn't appreciate the public display of solidarity. Feckless parents were the worst. Which was why he worried so much about getting it right himself. His actions now would affect Alfie for the rest of his life and that was a huge responsibility, one not to be taken lightly or disregarded without a second thought.

'Listen, this isn't about us or our absent parents but you can see for yourself that the decisions you make as a parent from here on in will have long, far-reaching consequences.'

'No pressure, then,' Anderson grumbled, his immaturity stubbornly shining through despite the pep talk.

'Which is why you don't want to be hasty, acting out without giving thought to the consequences of your actions.'

Where had Charlotte been when he'd needed to hear that straight talking? If he'd had someone like her on his team during those dark times, things could've been so very different. Maybe, just maybe he wouldn't have treated Sara and everyone else here with such reckless abandon.

'I don't want to spend the rest of my days here changing diapers. I want to go places.'

'The two aren't mutually exclusive, you know. There are plenty of dads on the team whose families are quite happy to move wherever the opportunities arise. Have you had a talk about the future, or what either of you want?' It seemed hypocritical to be dishing out advice on relationships when he'd never had a successful one of any kind himself but Hunter believed his failure made him the best person for the job. He'd been that idiot incapable of dealing with his emotions and was still dealing with the repercussions. A living example of what not to do.

At least Anderson had the grace to look ashamed. 'No. I guess I didn't take the news very well when she first told me and she isn't replying to any of my messages.'

Hunter groaned at the idiocy as history repeated itself. He might not have known Sara was pregnant but it was that same lack of communication that had killed their chances of being a family. That and his descent into the red mist that had consumed him and was now beckoning Anderson to the dark side.

Had he really been this self-absorbed when Sara had been making decisions about her future and that of their baby? Probably, and it was too late to apologise. He knew now the reason behind his own meltdown but it didn't excuse his behaviour and he took full responsibility for those he'd hurt. He bore many regrets but that one hurt the most.

Thankfully it wasn't too late for Gus and Maggie.

'Here's an idea, why don't you go and see her in person, prove you're taking this seriously and stop acting like a spoilt brat?' Insulting him was a risky move but there was no time for tiptoeing around him any more.

The slight nod in agreement enabled Hunter to speak freely without worrying he might lose a couple of teeth for his trouble.

'Do you love her?'

'Yes.' There was no hesitation, which gave some hope for the parents-to-be.

'Good. That's the foundation you need to start from. Concentrate on that for now. Find out if she feels the same and work together on taking that next step. A little word from the wise, you might want to quit the temper tantrums on ice too. You don't want her to think she has two babies to deal with and getting fired isn't going to help you, Maggie or the baby. Been there, lost my shirt and the girl. Don't recommend it.'

'You're right. I need to step up and be there for her.' He made to get out of the chair and it dawned on Hunter he meant now, wearing only a towel and still slightly slurring his words. Not the best impression to give if he wanted Maggie to forgive him and understand he was taking the matter seriously.

Hunter was quicker getting to his feet. He put a hand on Anderson's shoulder and firmly guided him back into his seat.

'It's late. She's probably asleep. I have a spare room you can stay the night in. Go see her tomorrow after you've sobered up.'

'I can probably give you some coaching in effective grovelling techniques before you see her, if it'll help?' Charlotte added her weight behind the campaign to get him back into Maggie's good books. They were turning out to be quite a team after all.

'It can't hurt. Thanks for all your help, guys.' Anderson threw his arms around Hunter, catching him around the waist in an awkward man hug.

'No problem. Just remember, we're your family too.' He took the hit so Charlotte wouldn't have to, hoping Gus would go to bed before he entered the 'I love you' stage of drunkenness.

Hunter knew he was in for a long sleepless night himself. Not only was he going to have to make frequent checks on his intoxicated patient but he had a lot of thinking to do about his own life. He couldn't very well preach the importance of communication one minute and pretend there hadn't been a shift between him and Charlotte the next.

If he followed his own advice and admitted he liked her, that there was a powerful attraction pulling them towards each other, then they'd have to discuss their next step too. The problem was if he let her into his life he was going to have to be honest about Alfie. Her reaction to that bombshell would determine what happened next.

Just as he'd told his fellow new dad, the time for playing games was over. They both had some growing up to do. These days a kiss meant much more than a kiss when it could potentially put the custody of his son at risk.

'Right, well, it's getting late. I should probably go home.' Charlotte waited until Hunter had safely ensconced his new lodger in the spare room before she made her excuses to leave.

There was no reason to hang around any longer than was necessary now her professional obligations had been fulfilled for the night and they appeared to be making progress with Gus. The biggest breakthrough for her, though, had been the sensitivity with which Hunter had handled everything. He'd given so much of himself tonight in the effort to get through to their teammate he'd really touched her heart. So much so she'd thought it a good idea to kiss him. Thank goodness for Anderson's intervention, which had averted the looming disaster.

If they had given in to whatever attraction had flickered in the moment there was no limit to the amount of damage it could have done, crossing the line of all her boundaries. She didn't want an atmosphere at work other than a professional one and didn't need any more complications that could impact on the team. It was a moment of madness she couldn't let happen again for her sake and everyone else's. That feeling of being out of control wasn't something she wanted to get used to.

'I'll walk you back to the arena so you can get your car.' Hunter was already holding the front door open for her, keen for her to hit the road.

'That's really not necessary. I'm a big girl. I can look after myself.' She'd been doing it for years and she couldn't afford to look any weaker than she already had tonight after almost kissing him.

He leaned against the door, arms folded. 'I know you can but do I really seem the sort of guy that'll stand here and watch a woman walk off into the darkness alone?'

No, he didn't. He was the perfect gentleman.

She didn't know when exactly she'd realised that after the low expectations she'd had about him. Probably around the time she'd been closing her eyes and waiting for him to kiss her.

He'd surprised her tonight with his level head and calm handling of the situation. Whilst that could only mean good things for his position with the Demons, it brought more concerns for her on a personal level. She was beginning to understand who he was beyond that hot-headed hunk who'd caught her eye and broken her teen heart. More so now he'd shared those deeply personal circumstances and given an insight as to what had been going on behind the scenes in the midst of his public meltdown.

She stepped out into the darkness and Hunter pulled the door shut behind them.

'What about Anderson? We shouldn't really leave him—' She tried one last time to put some distance between them so she had some space to put her feelings back in order. It didn't matter if Hunter Torrance was still a loose cannon or he'd turned out to be the nicest guy in the world, he had to remain off limits.

If only she could get her treacherous pounding heart to remember that every time he was near.

'He's snoring the house down already. I'm sure he won't miss me for ten minutes,' her escort insisted as he followed her down the path.

Even if she hadn't heard his heavy footsteps in the darkness, the hairs standing on the back of her neck alerted her to his presence as he caught up with her. She was doomed now to be at the mercy of her attraction whenever he was near. Not the best conditions to be working under. Together.

'I...er...think I have an apology to make. I judged you unfairly. If I'd known about your family situation... anyway, I shouldn't have been so horrible to you.' Although this being nice to each other didn't seem to be doing her any favours either. If anything, it was creating more problems for her.

'Don't worry about it. I'm used to it.'

That only increased her self-loathing for falling into line with all the other people who'd given him a hard time without just cause. She'd been there as that abandoned child and could easily have gone off the rails too. Perhaps having that one parent who'd loved her had been enough to save her from a complete breakdown when everything had gone wrong in her life. At least her mother had been there as a shoulder to cry on when she'd deemed herself unlovable, and had insisted it wasn't true. Hunter hadn't had anyone to allay his fears, only enforce them. With that little knowledge of his upbringing, it was amazing he'd ever been able to find his way back from the darkness, not that he'd ever succumbed to it.

'I know how much it hurts to be cast aside as if you're nothing. You should be proud of where you got to on your own.' She knew she was, whether her father cared or not.

'I am and ditto. If you don't mind me saying so, your dad sounds as much of a tool as mine.'

That made her laugh out loud, even though it was a sad state of affairs for them both. 'Yes, well, I try not to think about him too often.'

'Me either. Not any more. I'm all about the future these days and trying to leave the past behind.' They were walking into the car park now so she was able to see the determined set of his jaw under the arena lights. It was only natural she should wonder what, or who, that future should include.

They reached her vehicle and she found herself reluctant to end their chat, regardless of her subconscious urging her to jump in the car and hightail it out of there.

'That's definitely the healthier way to live, instead of letting old mistakes haunt you.' She'd been guilty of that on so many levels and she wasn't sure she'd ever really be free of her old ghosts. She had a growing admiration for Hunter, and his strength, if he'd truly been able to break free from his.

'Who would ever have imagined Hunter Torrance would become the spokesperson for common sense?' There was that self-deprecating smile, which almost had her sliding down the driver's door in hormonal appreciation. That mixture of handsome male and genuine good guy was too much for a girl to handle. It was usually one or the other and she didn't know how to defend against that kind of superpower combo.

'I think it did Anderson a world of good to hear it tonight. Hopefully it'll help him think clearly about his next step.' She appreciated the fact Hunter had shared those painful personal details in the hope their troubled friend would take something useful away from it. Not many would have, probably not even her unless he'd taken the lead first. It showed a real connection to the team on a personal level, which she'd doubted would ever happen.

'We made a good tag team tonight.'

'We did, didn't we?' She was smiling, proud of their joint achievement, as she made the mistake of looking up into his eyes. Her breath caught in her throat. In the aftermath of that last encounter she'd hoped she'd imagined that hunger but there it was again, flaring back to life and throwing her equilibrium into a death spiral.

'Perfect.' Hunter was focused on her soft lips tilted up towards him, beckoning him to find some comfort there after opening up old wounds. They'd both been hurt, they were both survivors and he was drawn to her more than ever before.

In that moment he was totally consumed by the need to kiss her and seal that connection once and for all. He watched her eyes close in anticipation and acceptance of his intention. There was no interruption this time, no one to prevent him from doing what came naturally.

It seemed to take for ever to close those few inches between them, as if he was moving in slow motion and preserving the memory of this first kiss for all time.

That soft cushion of her lips against his was a relief; a

pleasure he'd been denying himself for some time, but soon even that wasn't enough. He wanted more, he wanted to taste her, to lose himself in her, and that's when he knew he was in trouble. If they'd stood here until daybreak, the kissing lasting until morning dew glistened in their hair, it would've ended too soon. There was a red flag waving somewhere in the distance, making sure he didn't stray too far into deep waters. That future he was so determined to get right for him and his boy didn't include anyone else in the picture.

He broke away and swivelled around to glance back in the direction of his house. 'I should probably get back to my house guest.'

Kissing Charlotte had given him that same rush of testosterone that accounted for every minute of his time in the penalty box. It was that feeling of doing what he needed to do in that moment, of being true to the man he was, and stuff the rules. He'd worked hard to regain his self-control and this set a dangerous precedent. Especially when he couldn't bring himself to regret a second of it. His whole future here was based on his repentance for similar rash decisions.

He was sure Charlotte was as confused as he was about what was happening. Regardless of her initial hurry to get away, she'd been into that kiss as much as he had. A woman like her didn't need a complication like him messing up her orderly life but there was no denying the chemistry. They'd tried doing that and it had landed them here, making out in the middle of the car park, but anything more than this would be bad news for both of them.

She nodded, probably coming to the same conclusion.

He only got a few steps away before she called after him. 'Hunter? You don't have a girlfriend, do you?'

'No, I don't have a girlfriend, Charlotte.'

'I...er...saw you waving to someone in the stands tonight. I thought maybe—'

'I'm not with anyone. I'm not in the habit of cheating.' There was an edge to his tone but it felt like a step backwards to be accused of two-timing already.

'Right. A friend, then?'

'Goodnight, Charlotte.'

It was all he was giving her for tonight. So far he wasn't doing a very good job of resisting temptation and prioritising his son over his love life. In his defence, he hadn't planned any of this but that didn't mean he was sorry, or that he would follow it up.

Alfie was his personal business. Tonight's journey to find Anderson had been a matter of professional survival. At first. Somewhere in between those chats Charlotte had created a whole new section of his life to worry about.

She was smart, funny, beautiful, not afraid to show her emotions and up until tonight he'd been darned sure she'd hated his guts. He'd never expected her to be responsive to his advances unless it came in the form of a fist to his face. Although the impact had been pretty much the same.

Charlotte wasn't like other women he'd known. She didn't care for the man who'd played in the NHL or spent longer in the penalty box than the entire national team. Now she'd taken the time to get to know him, or as much as he'd allow, it was certainly an ego boost to find someone who liked him without the fame or notoriety. However, there was the worry that one kiss had just blown apart all the careful planning of his new life when all he could think about as he walked away was recapturing the moment.

Indeed, it was probably a small blessing he'd been lumbered with the Demons' resident troublemaker for the night or they might never have left his place. The next few hours on vomit watch would give him the space to think about what he'd done and what he was going to do about it, if anything.

He wasn't ready to share Alfie with her. It was too early to say, *Oh, yeah, here's my kid. I'm trying to get custody. I'm sure you'll make a great stand-in mom.* That wasn't fair to anyone on the back of one kiss. Neither did he want to jeopardise his chances of getting custody by flaunting a new relationship in front of the grieving O'Reillys or upsetting Alfie. He was going to have to tread very carefully now he was no longer free to behave however it suited him. Everything he did had consequences for those around him—he'd learned that the hard way and he wasn't about to make the same mistakes over again.

CHAPTER FOUR

CHARLOTTE WAS AT the rink bright and early and long before any training was due to start, with her own skates slung over her shoulder. She hadn't cut it as a hockey player herself but she could skate. The lessons had been her weekly escape from the rows and the tears of her unhappy home life.

The first skate of the day on unsullied ice always helped her unwind and unclutter her mind and she needed that more than ever this morning. There was so much to process and a lot more she needed to work through with Hunter. Despite pulling rank yesterday, they'd worked better in a partnership to get to the bottom of Anderson's diva fever and there was still a long way to go to get him back on top form. A child was supposed to be a lifelong commitment, not a problem that could, or should, be *fixed* overnight. He would need sustained support as he came to terms with the big changes in his life.

Then, of course, there was also the whole kissing Hunter thing. She was trying to work out if it had been a one-off, caused by working too closely outside office hours, or if the fire would still burn inside them both in the cold light of day. Hence the early start and restless legs. There were all sorts of implications in getting involved with a co-worker and there were risks involved she wasn't yet sure she wanted to take, no matter how tender his touch or how much she wanted more.

Unfortunately, as she made her way towards the ice it seemed she wasn't the only one to arrive early. Shouts echoed around the arena along with the sound of blades cutting through her fresh ice. She stashed her skates away until she could manage some alone time here again. This wasn't the start to the day she'd anticipated, especially as she realised the two men who'd gatecrashed her quiet morning were the same ones who'd kept her up late last night. Hunter and Anderson were so focused on their drills they didn't appear to notice they had a spectator.

Even the sight of the man with whom she'd been in a passionate clinch only hours ago gave her system a jolt to rival her early shot of caffeine. A shiver danced a merry jig along her spine at the memory of his hands there whilst his lips had caressed hers. He was a man of many fine skills.

Although he was no longer a professional player he'd certainly maintained his fitness level and she was sure he had the body to show for it. Damn it if she couldn't stop thinking about that image as her eyes followed him powering along the full length of the rink.

It took a lot of self-discipline to stay in that great a shape, even if his past antics had caused her to question it. He was still that mesmerising figure she'd never been able to take her eyes off during a game.

Hunter dropped his stick to the ice and rounded up the pucks littered around him. One by one he and his partner whacked them into the back of the net with such ferocity Charlotte was convinced they'd lodge in the advertising hoardings. It wasn't until he was skating back towards the centre that he caught sight of her on the sideline.

'Hey. I didn't see you come in.' He seemed pleased to see her if the bone-melting grin was any indication.

It was a sign that he might have seen last night as more than a spur-of-the-moment mistake and while that felt good, it meant she might have to make some decisions on what it was she wanted to happen next. She'd sworn she wouldn't cross that line with him, only to find herself entwined with him moments later. A physical attraction was one thing but working alongside him, getting to know him, took any further shenanigans into the realms of a relationship. That was something she didn't jump into easily when too-vivid visions of her parents' messy divorce made her wary of getting in too deep with anyone, never mind a man known for his unreliability in the past. Still, she was a woman who knew how to protect her heart. She just didn't let anyone in.

'Slaying some demons, are we?' She tipped her head towards his training partner, who was more focused than he'd been when she'd seen him last time. He'd barely been able to walk then, never mind balance the weight of his bulk on two sharp blades.

'One or two. What about you? Are you up for an early morning session?'

It was an entirely innocent remark. If he'd meant to conjure up a picture of the two of them lolling around in bed on a lazy Sunday morning he would've said it with a wink and an intention to make her blush.

'I'm, uh, just here to get a few things from the office.' Skating was something she did for herself and not something she was ready to share with him. It was her private pleasure, and no longer a team pursuit. After witnessing Hunter's drills, she wasn't sure he'd understand that distinction.

Anderson acknowledged her with a nod. 'I think I'll hit the showers. I have a lot to do today.'

Left alone with Hunter in his old Demons shirt she

wasn't prepared for the memories it brought back of him at his best, including last night when he'd had her in his arms. It was too early in the morning to be dealing with raging hormones, too scary to start examining what the hell was happening and definitely too public to find out what came next.

'That's one way to get Anderson to work out his frustrations but I don't want him to think brute strength is the answer to all his problems.' It might work in hockey but he was going to need to adopt a gentler, more methodical approach to his personal life.

He cocked his head to one side, a smirk playing across his lips. 'Are you calling me a brute?'

Charlotte gulped. *Brute* conjured up all sorts of primitive connotations she certainly didn't need to associate with him when she was already having trouble controlling herself around him.

'With the penalty minutes you've clocked up over the years, some might say *brute* was appropriate.'

'Ouch.'

It was a low blow but she'd do whatever it took to put an end to this apparent flirting. She couldn't cope with it. Wobbly knees would destroy the illusion she was confident about what she was doing here and turn her into Bambi on ice instead.

'I see Anderson's almost human today.' She changed the subject, using Anderson as a buffer for this unresolved sexual tension between them. He was the poster child for bad judgement and rash decisions. She was probably one more Hunter clinch away from an epic breakdown of equipment-smashing proportions and she didn't even know it.

Once she'd pulled the brakes on the hot and meaningful exchanged glances, Hunter followed suit and put a bit more space between them.

'I think we've made some progress. He has some work to do but it was his decision to get started early and make up some ground today. I do know he's serious about getting back on track with the club.'

'Gray will be happy.'

'That might be overstating it but at least there's a chance he'll think again about getting people fired.'

'That's a win all round, then. It's good to start the day on a high. I'll check in with Anderson later and see how he's getting on. I need to take a look at those stitches again anyway.' It wasn't that she didn't trust Hunter's word but she wanted to see, and speak to, Anderson herself to gauge his mood. She wanted to be optimistic about his future as well as her own but she was also a realist. That sort of behaviour wasn't often cured overnight and she, along with Gray, would still be watching him with a careful eye.

'Be my guest.'

'Right, I have a few things to sort out for Nottingham so I should go.' She was already making her way towards the exit and away from trouble.

'You're being hopeful. We still have an away match to win before we get there.'

'I like to be organised.' It wasn't that she was overly optimistic about their chances. A hockey fan through and through, she'd booked her flights for the Final Four Weekend long before Hunter had come on the scene. She would be there no matter who made it to the finals and if the Demons were there it would be all the sweeter.

The doctor didn't usually travel with the team but she'd be happy to combine work with pleasure. Except now it would mean she and Hunter would be spending more time together in close proximity. If they carried on from where they'd left off last night there was a danger it would all burn out of control and she knew better than to let her heart overrule her head.

He didn't try to stop her leaving, for which she was grateful. One more romantic recall into his arms and she knew they'd be melting the very ground they were standing on. She'd used up her quota of bravado in walking away and she would make sure she left enough time for Mr Torrance to have packed up his kit before she ventured out of the office again and risked another pulse-racing encounter. He was just too much excitement for this sleepy town and always had been.

She grabbed what she needed from the filing cabinet and was ready to leave when the sound of running water coming from somewhere nearby alerted her to the fact she wasn't alone.

'Anderson, is that you?' she called out before she entered the changing room, as she always did so anyone who wished to preserve their modesty could do so. Not that they were usually shy about parading in the buff. She was sure they'd done it on purpose in those early days just to get her flustered but she was used to it now. Men's naked bodies were part of the fixtures around here.

The shower shut off and she hoped to goodness he covered up before he came out to speak to her. A serious conversation about his state of mind would go more smoothly if she wasn't worried about a lapse in eye contact.

'I…uh…just wanted to see you…er…to make sure you were all right after last night.'

'Do you make a habit of dropping in on the players when they're in the showers?' A bemused Hunter, not Anderson, padded out barefoot and double-towelled, with one around his waist and another in his hand, drying his hair.

Holy six pack!

She was sure her mouth was dropping open and closed

like a sea creature stranded on the shore, fighting for survival. Eventually she forced herself to speak before he felt it his duty to come and give her mouth to mouth.

'I don't get my kicks spying on naked hockey players, thank you very much.' Only ex-hockey players.

'Oh, yes, we're much too *brutish* for you, aren't we?' He tossed the hair-drying towel aside and she was finding difficulty coming up with an argument, or even why she wanted one as he walked towards her.

'If we're talking sexy Canadian stereotypes I'm more a Gilbert Blythe kind of girl,' she lied, wanting to focus on someone the opposite of the muscle-bound hunk advancing on her. It would be dangerous to admit to the attraction here, alone in a small room with Hunter naked except for a scrap of white fabric.

'I'll start calling you Carrots, then, shall I?' He had every right to look pleased with himself when he'd just scored extra hottie points.

'You know *Anne of Green Gables*?' Now she came to think of it, he did resemble her other teenage fantasy boyfriend with his dark wavy hair and that accent that made every *Sorry* impossible to forgive.

'Read it, and watched the mini-series as an essential part of getting inside the female psyche at an early age. I even wore a flat cap for a while.' He smiled bashfully at the memory and Charlotte couldn't help but sigh out loud.

'Yes, well, we're all older, wiser and much more cynical these days.'

'Perhaps, but there's always room for a little romance, don't you think?' He was doing it again, staring at her with such naked lust it took her breath away.

She was doing her best to remain strong and avoid falling too quickly under his spell again but her mouth was dry with want. A droplet of water fell from the ends of his

tousled hair and she watched it with the thirst of a travel-
ler lost in the desert, searching for that life-giving oasis. It
splashed onto his shoulder and trickled over the muscular
planes of his chest, its journey gaining momentum over
the smooth skin, unimpeded until it reached that trail of
dark hair from navel to...

Oh. He'd caught her staring.

'Do you shave?' It was the first thing that popped into
her head so she said it to divert her thoughts from where
they were headed. Except she hadn't given any thought to
where her gaze was lingering.

His taut belly moved with his laughter. 'No. Do you?'

She frowned, not quite understanding his meaning. Did
he think she had a hairy chest? Then the penny dropped
and she wished the ground would too.

'I didn't mean... I was talking about your chest. I wasn't
staring at your...'

She so was.

He cleared his throat, clearly as embarrassed as she was
by her staring. She would've imagined someone with his
history would've been used to it and that lack of arrogance
only added to his appeal for her. There was nothing more
off-putting than a man who was fully aware of his looks
and used them to his advantage.

'About last night—'

'I'll leave you to get dressed. I only came in to get a few
things.' She could tell he was gearing up to give her the
brush-off. If he'd wanted anything more they wouldn't be
standing here, making small talk, while he was dressed in
nothing but a towel. Until this second she hadn't realised
it was her who didn't want this to be over already.

'Wait.' He grabbed hold of her arm, pulled her back so
they were almost nose to nose, his hot breath mingling with

hers. His freshly soaped skin was warm and wet against hers, reminding her he was *au naturel* below that towel.

'What are we doing, Hunter?' This was her chance to reclaim control. If she truly wanted to prevent this from happening she should've been pushing him away, not welcoming his touch as though she'd been waiting for it all her life.

'Probably something really, really stupid.' At least Hunter was acknowledging that he was also powerless against this attraction as he took her in his arms.

Any fight left her at that first contact and she surrendered to the next. There was something more urgent in his kiss this time, matching her need to make up for lost time. As if the pressure of fighting these feelings had finally been too much and had exploded in a frenzy of body parts desperate to connect.

His tongue courted hers and with his two hands planted firmly on her backside, he pulled her closer, leaving her in no doubt about how much he wanted her. He was as hard for her as she was wet for him, their mutual appreciation reaching critical levels.

Her carefully layered shirt and sweater combo, chosen to keep her body temperature regulated for skating purposes, now seemed excessive for this increasingly hot interlude. Arousal coursed through her veins, reaching her every nerve ending until she was nothing but a mass of erogenous zones.

He was the only man capable of making her act this recklessly but she wasn't so far gone she was prepared to lose her inhibitions in public. It definitely wouldn't aid her career if the team doctor was to be discovered getting passionate with the half-naked physio in the locker room.

'This is a mistake. Someone could walk in at any time. You were right. This is a stupid idea.'

'Charlotte, wait!' Hunter could only watch as she bolted from the building. It would only cause more of a scene if he ran after her, his towel at half-mast around his waist.

He did, however, dress as quickly, and as cautiously, as he could without causing serious injury to himself as he waited for the after-effects of their unexpected, extremely hot tryst to wear off.

So much for careful planning and taking things slowly. Apparently his impulsive side hadn't left him altogether, although he would deny any man not to respond as primitively as he had to the hungry way she'd stared at his body. Her emotions were as easy to read now as they had been that first day they'd met and she'd made no attempt to disguise her contempt for him.

After Sara and the years he'd missed of Alfie's life he preferred knowing where he stood. No good came of secrets and that went for him too. He'd deliberated telling her about Alfie's existence when he'd been unsure last night had been anything other than a moment of weakness. Given this morning's events and the persistent frequency of the tightness in his jeans, the chemistry with Charlotte was rapidly invading all areas of his life.

He might be wary of inviting someone to share his most personal, private secrets but if her hasty exit was anything to go by, so was Charlotte. It was important she knew they were braving this strange new land together.

She didn't seem the type to engage in passionate embraces on a whim; she wasn't one of the puck bunnies who'd kill to be in that position with a player in the locker room. If she was he would've heard about it by now. Players weren't known for their discretion on such matters. Then again, until recently he hadn't been the settling-down type whose only goal was a steady cheque to pay a mortgage. People weren't always who they appeared to be but he trusted his instincts. She was the first woman he'd had time for since finding out about his son and that had to mean something, something he was keen to explore.

He chased her down to the car park and called after her. 'Can we at least talk about this?'

Apparently not as her little silver hatchback screeched away from the arena.

For someone who spent most of her spare time at the arena, Charlotte did a good job of eluding Hunter until the night of their away match and even then she'd driven rather than taken a seat on the team bus. Something that hadn't gone unnoticed by the others, who'd wondered what had caused her to forsake her free ride when she normally insisted on travelling, despite the away team providing their own medical support. Hunter had simply kept his head down and muttered something about her having other errands to run. It wasn't as if he could put his hands up and say it was his fault she wanted to be on her own. That he'd made her act as irresponsibly as he once had and now she regretted it.

He felt the need to apologise the minute he cast his eyes on her, even though they hadn't done anything wrong. Under the fluorescent lights of a jam-packed concourse probably wasn't the ideal spot to confront what had happened but she hadn't left him much option when she kept dodging him.

'Charlotte, you have to talk to me at some point. I'm sorry if I made you uncomfortable but we still have to work together.' There wasn't much hope for more than that since a couple of kisses had sent her scurrying into the shadows.

They were jostled by the stampeding crowds keen to get their pre-game snacks and drinks from the nearby concession stands. Hunter took her by the elbow and gently led her to a corner where there was considerably less footfall and noise going on around them.

'Did anyone see us? In the changing room, I mean.' The events had clearly been at the forefront of her mind when she launched into her fears immediately, rather than continuing to dance around the subject.

'No. Our secret's safe.' He only managed a half-smile at the thought of being someone's dirty little secret. For her sake he wanted to laugh it off, pretend the matter wasn't of any great significance so they could move on past it. In reality, though, he would rather be someone Charlotte was proud to be seen with regardless of what people thought. Not being reminded that he was still the man no one wished to be associated with.

'Good.' A delicate blush stained her skin but it was difficult to tell if it was through embarrassment or heat at the memory. He knew which one would be easier for him to stomach.

'Charlotte—'

'Hunter—'

They stumbled over each other attempting to address the chasm that had opened up between them after their latest indiscretion. In ordinary circumstances making out should have spelled the beginning of a relationship, not the end of one. It might be wishful thinking on his part but he was holding onto the small hope it was circumstance alone that had caused Charlotte's sudden retreat from him.

'I'm sorry if I put you in a compromising position at work but, for the record, we haven't done anything wrong.' They'd only done what had come naturally, albeit at the wrong time and in the wrong place.

She glanced around, obviously still skittish about getting caught even when the passers-by were more interested in getting to their seats before the puck dropped than two people freaked out by their attraction to one another. 'I know... It's just... I wasn't expecting this.'

He understood her fears, he had reservations himself, but for altogether different reasons. Whilst she might be concerned she'd be nothing more than a notch on his bedpost, he feared the opposite.

'Neither was I. We can take things at whatever pace you want.' One thing was for sure, it was impossible to walk away and pretend nothing was happening.

She studied him closely, as if she was trying to work out if he was spinning her a line or he was being genuine. That hurt more than she could ever have imagined.

'It's not only what nearly happened, or could happen between us that I'm worried about. I don't know you, not really.' This was a very different woman from the one who'd been in his arms not long ago, a cautious Charlotte who probably didn't make a habit of the sort of behaviour he'd been famous for.

He couldn't blame her. They'd taken a risk of being spotted, of being ridiculed or, worse, sacked on the spot. Sara's parents would've had a field day with the news and then he'd have had to explain to his son why he'd screwed up their future together for a woman he'd just met. Only he knew he wouldn't have put either his or Charlotte's livelihoods at risk for something trivial and it was frustrating he couldn't get that point across.

'Now, how can we rectify that if you won't be in the same room as me? Hmm?' He tilted his head to one side and gave her his best hound dog impression so she'd stop seeing him as some sort of threat.

That earned him a soft, sweet laugh. 'So you found the flaw in my total avoidance ploy, huh?'

Hunter sucked a breath in through his teeth. 'Not the most practical tactic when we do play for the same team.'

'Always thinking about the long game and not the interim strategy, that's me.' The skin at the corners of her eyes creased with laughter, a most welcome sight after an anxious few days of silence.

'Sometimes it does you good to act on impulse and not worry about what happens further down the line.'

'And how did that work out for you?'

He'd been talking about letting their attraction win out over common sense but Charlotte's raised eyebrow suggested another nod back at his hockey days.

'I said sometimes. Not as a lifestyle choice. Sometimes the most spontaneous moments can bring the greatest pleasure.' He lowered his voice so his next words were for her ears only. 'I have many regrets, Charlotte, but kissing you will never be one of them.'

If it wasn't for the constant stream of people nudging past he would be tempted to do it again.

He was running the risk of scaring her off again by being so blatant about his desires but it was going to take at least one of them being honest if there was a chance of repeating the experience.

'Hunter... I...'

He watched her gulp and swallow, struggling to form a reply, and waited patiently for the verdict on his gamble.

The klaxon sounded from deep inside the arena, signalling the end of the pre-game warm-up and penetrating their bubble. The teams would be making their way off the ice after their drills and stretches to prepare for the game behind the scenes. Where he and Charlotte should be.

'We really need to hustle our backsides down there before Gray starts on the warpath.' She turned away from him, timing, as ever, against them.

Hunter mused over whether or not to force this conversation to its conclusion so he would know once and for all where he stood with her. She was driving him crazy. Since it had taken this long to pin her down he figured it wouldn't help matters to put her job in jeopardy again by making her tardy.

'We wouldn't want that but, believe me, I'm still keen on that getting to know each other idea.'

Charlotte almost fell down the steps at Hunter's insistence they pick up where they'd left off. Especially when his hand was at her back, escorting her towards the changing rooms and heating her skin with the warmth of his touch. She'd been stupid to think a few days and some distance from him would put any lustful thoughts out of her head. One glimpse of him, a promise of more of the same and her willpower had dissolved.

It had been all too tempting to ignore her duty to the players and the team in favour of spending time with him again. The very reason she'd beaten herself up over the last time they'd lost track of where, and who, they were. When she was with him nothing else seemed to matter and that was dangerous when she was putting her job at risk for a man she barely knew beyond how good his lips felt on hers. She didn't know where they went from here and she certainly didn't want to have to commit to anything if it left her position on the team vulnerable, so she was glad she'd been buzzed out of her reverie in the nick of time.

They were lucky that Gray hadn't missed them either and they were able to merge back into the team preparations as if nothing had happened. On the outside at least. Her insides were having difficulty catching up with her logical brain, still fluttering and unsettled by being so close to Hunter.

At least being squashed in behind the bench as a stowaway on the away side meant they were most definitely in a crowd and close enough to the action to keep their minds where they were supposed to be—on the ice.

'Anderson seems to have recovered form. Good job, you two.' There was a brief nod from Gray as the player stretched his legs, skating rings around the opposition in the opening minutes of the game.

He didn't ask what was behind the transformation, more concerned with results than the journey, and neither Charlotte nor Hunter volunteered the information. She knew from her subsequent conversations with him that he and Maggie were trying to work things out and that in itself had improved his mood and his play, but Anderson's private life was exactly that and unless he chose to share the details of his recent troubles, they would remain confidential.

She and Hunter exchanged smiles over the pat on the back from their leader before he went back to discussing tactics with the rest of his men. Their joint effort with Anderson certainly appeared to have yielded favourable results and she could see Hunter stood a little taller with the recognition. She couldn't help but wonder how long it had been since someone had actually congratulated him on a job well done.

For a long time he'd probably endured nothing but negativity and scepticism over his work ethic and she was as guilty as everyone else who'd refused to give him a break. So wrapped up in her own thoughts and feelings about how she'd been affected by his presence here, she'd given virtually no thought to the positive addition he'd *actually* been to the team. Perhaps it was self-preservation. She didn't need any more reason to like him when he was already sidestepping around those work-colleague boundaries.

The volume levels of the crowd rose around her at a skirmish out by the Demons' goal as they went all out to defend. It was hard to see what was going on through the throng of bodies vying for prominence. Suddenly there was a cry for the medic. As the crowd parted and anxious players called for help, it became obvious there was something seriously wrong. One body remained prone on the ice, the area around him rapidly turning scarlet with blood. It was Colton, the Demons' winger.

Hunter swore, grabbed a towel and had vaulted over the bench before she'd even taken her first step onto the rink. Two Demons players arrived either side of her and escorted her quickly over to the scene so she didn't slip on the ice.

'Ambulance. Now!' she shouted to the Cobras' medical staff, who were making their way over too. The amount of blood spurting from Colton's leg told of the severity of the injury and this was no time for territory marking.

'It's an artery.' Hunter dropped to his knees and held the towel to the deep gash across the thigh, probably caused by the blade of someone's skate in the melee.

'Keep applying the pressure. Colton? We need to try and elevate this leg.' In such circumstances there was always a chance of a patient bleeding to death as the blood was pumping so quickly from the heart and a cut artery was a time-critical wound. Everything she and Hunter did now to stem the flow of blood could determine whether or not he survived.

'Charlotte?' Hunter directed her attention to the once-white towel, which was now a bright red, infused with their patient's blood. It would only take losing two pints of blood before he went into shock. There was no more time to waste.

'Give me your belt.' She didn't even wait for a response and simply helped herself. Despite the adrenaline pumping in her own veins and the struggle to keep her breathing regulated in the midst of the drama, her fingers worked nimbly to unbuckle his belt.

She tugged him roughly towards her and whipped the strip of leather from around his waist. All the time he kept pressure on the wound without blinking an eye at her, as if having bossy women strip him was an everyday occurrence. Or he knew exactly what she was doing. The belt made a perfect tourniquet around the thigh and she pulled it just tight enough to hopefully slow the bleeding but not cut off total supply to the limb.

'Nicely done, Doctor.' Hunter offered his support with a smile and a wink. He was the one grounding source for her in the midst of the drama. It was a comfort knowing that she wasn't in this alone.

'You too, Mr Torrance. Now let's get you to hospital, Colton.'

It was only as they rushed off the ice towards the waiting ambulance that the uneasy silence around the arena became noticeable. Everyone had been waiting with bated breath to see the fate of the injured player. It didn't matter what side he was on when there was a life at stake. She was glad she hadn't felt that weight of expectation on her shoulders as she'd worked and that had been down to Hunter's assistance. It wasn't that she couldn't treat this sort of injury solo—after all, that was the nature of her job here. No, it was simply...reassuring for someone to have her back.

She relayed all the relevant information to the paramedics so they could radio ahead to the hospital and prep for surgery. With Hunter still taking charge of wound pressure, they both climbed into the vehicle alongside their patient.

'We need oxygen, double cannula and get fluids started.' She was talking to herself as much as anyone else in the vicinity so she had all bases covered.

The back of an ambulance made for a small workspace

and she couldn't help but brush against Hunter with every bump in the road as she inserted the cannulas into Colton's hands.

'Sorry,' she said as they went around a corner and she was forced to brace herself against Hunter's frame to steady herself. It was more important to get the IV and much-needed pain relief up and running than continue her ill-conceived avoid-body-contact-with-Hunter plan.

'No problem.'

She didn't take her eyes off her patient but she could feel the warmth of Hunter's slow grin on her back. It made her shiver all the same.

'Will I make it back for the final period, Doc?' The pale Colton was trying to sit up and displaying that hockey-player spirit that demanded to see the game out, no matter what. On this occasion she was definitely going to have to disappoint him.

'I'm afraid not. You're going to have to go straight into Theatre to have that artery stitched.' She wasn't even sure if they'd finish the match after that scare.

'Even Gray should understand you missing the rest of the game. I don't think he'll be docking your wages this once.' Hunter attempted to soften the blow and she appreciated it. It probably aided Colton's compliance to have a kindred spirit on board, someone who knew from personal experience how it felt to be left on the sidelines.

'But I'll be okay to play in the finals?' The pleading eyes were begging for reassurance but Charlotte didn't have it in her to lie, even to a seriously injured man.

'Don't worry about that for now. First things first. We need to get you into Theatre. We're almost at the hospital now.' They'd done as much as they could for Colton but her mind would be much more at ease when she knew the surgeon was doing his bit to save his life too.

'I'll phone Gray as soon as we arrive and let him know you're keen to get back ASAP.' Hunter wasn't making him any promises other than to relay a progress report but he was providing that extra reassurance she was beginning to realise she could count on. Even though they both knew Colton was probably finished for the season, there was no need to give him more reason to worry before he went into surgery.

It wasn't until they'd handed over their patient into the hands of the hospital staff that Charlotte was able to take time for some deep fortifying breaths. She could only watch, her stomach in knots, as he was stretchered away down the corridor at high speed, her part in ensuring his survival over for now.

'Wow. That was a rush.'

It seemed she wasn't the only one coming down from the adrenaline high as Hunter let out an unsteady breath next to her.

'Not one I'm in a hurry to experience again, thanks.' Now she had time and space to think about events, the enormity of the undertaking was beginning to hit home.

A chill penetrated her bones and set her knees trembling. She practically fell into one of the chairs lining the corridor.

'Your first life-or-death emergency?' Hunter landed in the seat next to her with a heavy thud and she could see he wasn't unaffected by the drama either. It was a comfort to see her reaction was totally normal.

She nodded. Her eyes were already beginning to well up as emotion built inside her and she didn't trust herself to talk without her voice cracking. They'd very nearly lost one of their own tonight and the responsibility of keeping him alive had rested heavily on her shoulders. It was the nature of the path she'd chosen but her work in sports therapy tended more towards joint and muscle problems than life-threatening crises. Tonight had been a sobering reminder of the serious commitment she'd made to her career and the team.

'Mine too.' He reached across and squeezed her hand. It was the closest she'd get to the hug she needed right now.

She swallowed the unprofessional tears away since she was the one who'd actually trained for this and focused on the fact Colton was alive.

'You certainly seemed to know what you were doing back there.' As she recalled, he'd applied pressure to the wound area before she'd even told him to.

'Well, I do have some training in the field. I was at medical school briefly before I decided to toss it all in for hockey.'

Her eyes widened at that new information. 'Ah. So the physiotherapy didn't totally come out of left field? You could easily have been Dr Hunter Torrance?'

'Medicine was definitely something I was interested in pursuing. Actually, I'm not sure which career was more about rebelling against my parents.'

'Your relationship with them was that strained?'

He nodded solemnly. 'I was adopted and always made very aware of the fact. Told I should be grateful they'd taken me on. At eighteen I decided to find my birth parents, only to be rejected again. They didn't want me any more then than when I was born. Becoming a doctor would've stuck it to those who thought I would never amount to anything but the idea of being a hockey player... well, it was glamorous and exciting and something I knew they'd envy. Until I screwed it all up, of course.'

It was her turn to squeeze back. 'Don't be so hard on yourself. We've all had our struggles. Yours just happened to be very public.'

Her heart broke for his younger self who'd so obviously been hurting and searching for acceptance. She was able to see that explosive behaviour in a different light now she knew it had been more than bad temper at play and forgave him every wrong he'd done in her eyes. Not only had he been dealing with that loneliness and isolation of his personal circumstances but he'd been demonised by the press and disappointed fans. Even when he'd shown up, full of remorse, she'd clung onto her own grudge and dismissed his claims. It only added to the injustice done to him and to the guilt she was feeling as a result.

If she imagined her trials and tribulations with her parents playing out in arenas around the country she doubted she would have recovered as effectively as he had. When he'd turned up professing to have changed his life she'd assumed sports medicine was second best, the closest he could get to the ice without playing again. That the Demons' medical staff was the consolation prize when it had been the jackpot to her. To find out he had that calling to help others ingrained in him after all challenged her preconceived ideas about his character and stripped away some of those fears about getting involved with him.

She was fast running out of excuses to avoid her feelings, leaving only the outright terror at the thought of putting her heart on the line again. What if she gave it away only to find it cast aside like an unwanted toy when something, someone better came along? She hadn't been enough for her father to stick around and she didn't want to put herself in the position again of letting someone else have so much control over her emotions or her life.

The only certainty she had with Hunter tonight was there would be no escape from these growing feelings for him until they knew for sure Colton had pulled through.

CHAPTER FIVE

HUNTER WASN'T USED to being the one receiving pats on the back or hand squeezes and he couldn't decide if the squirming in his seat was because he was uneasy over it or *too* comfortable with it. It seemed as though he was finally finding his feet as part of the team. More than that, he and Charlotte had formed their own partnership. Not so long ago professional courtesy would've been all he'd wanted from her but they'd gone way beyond that point. He wouldn't have shared details of his personal life with the same woman who'd turned her nose up at him when they'd first met. There had definitely been a shift in their dynamic and it wasn't only down to the random bouts of kissing.

'You didn't do so badly under the spotlight tonight. Actually, you were kind of amazing out there.' The way she'd handled the situation so calmly and efficiently had shown everyone this was so much more than a job to her. She was dedicated to the team but also a medical professional whom any man could trust with his life. Maybe even with the knowledge of his son.

'We're good together.' Her coy smile suggested she was thinking about more than their time in the cramped confines of the ambulance.

'That we are, and if I recall there was a promise made

about getting to know each other a little better.' It was as important to him to be upfront and honest about what this was as it was for her. A relationship for him now was always going to include someone else and he was done with secrets.

'Well, we've made a start. I had no idea about your time in medical school.'

'That makes it your turn for the Q and A. Let's start with an easy one. Why the Demons? What made you join the team?' He wanted to know everything that made her tick so he could work out what it was that kept putting obstacles in their path. Even if he ignored the comings and goings of the staff and patients flooding through the emergency department and stole another kiss from her, he knew she'd be running again by tomorrow.

'I've been into hockey since the arena opened.'

'A real fan, then?' He knew she enjoyed hockey nights, he'd seen it, but he hadn't realised her love of the game had come before her role on the team.

'You could say that,' she muttered under her breath, but he could see no reason why she'd be embarrassed by it.

At a time when most young girls would've been more interested in fashion and make-up, she'd committed her time to a sport that wasn't for the faint-hearted. It explained so much about her character.

'That must've been around the time I played here?' He did the mental calculations. The chances were he'd seen her in passing at one time or another.

'Yeah.' Her embarrassment continued to flare a crimson contrast to her porcelain skin, the same flushed look she had every time he kissed her.

'It's kinda hot, knowing you're a *real* hockey fan.' He wanted to reach out and tilt her chin up to look at him and make that connection again but he didn't. An invisible barrier had been hastily erected since their last moment of weakness but he thought he could break it down again with a hit of honesty. Hockey had been his life and it was a new experience having someone who understood that commitment and passion.

He'd screwed up his own career but his love of the game had never diminished. That was why he'd jumped at the chance Gray had given him to work here. He could've come over, set up his own practice and eventually built up a client list, but as the Demons' physio he got a chance to recapture that passion. Now he could do that with Charlotte too if she would only let him.

'I'm a Demon through and through.' She sighed as if it was a bad thing when he'd seen her loyalty as a positive. It gave them more common ground other than this mutual attraction they were having difficulty with.

'Good. I'm sure Gray's glad he'll never have to worry about losing you to a rival team.'

'You don't understand,' she said, her downcast gaze giving him sudden reason for concern. He wasn't used to her being so cagey with him. Usually she was very vocal with her opinion.

'So why don't you tell me what it is that's bothering you?' He wanted to understand so they could move past whatever was causing this stumbling block between them. If she couldn't share this obviously personal problem with him, it was going to be very difficult to confide in her about his son. Trust was a two-way street for him.

She took a deep breath, refilling her lungs and doing nothing to allay his worries that there was a serious problem here. 'I'll admit I wasn't the *kindest* person to you on meeting for the first time but I, uh, might've held a bit of a grudge against you.'

'Oh?' It didn't come as any great surprise but he was interested to know the reasons behind it.

'Well…you kinda ruined my life.'

They were the words Hunter had always expected to hear from someone but they still hit hard. He didn't know what he'd done to Charlotte to deserve them but he wasn't in any doubt that he did. After all, ruining people's lives was what he'd done best before he'd turned his own around.

He was staring at her as if she'd gone stark raving mad. Maybe she finally had. It would explain why she was about to spill her biggest, most humiliating secret but it was now or never. She couldn't avoid this any more when he was opening up to her and showing he was just as human and flawed as she was. Perhaps after this confession, whatever the outcome, she'd finally be able to move on from that chapter of her life. As long as he kept the story to himself and saved her from prolonged mortification.

She gulped in another breath and prepared to unload her greatest shame. In the middle of a busy hospital, waiting for news on the fate of one of their players for goodness' sake. She was beginning to think she should've told the whole sorry story from the outset and saved herself a whole heap of trouble. After this bombshell he wouldn't be so keen to get up close and personal with her.

'It might sound dramatic but teenage girls are, and when the one thing they love falls apart their whole world collapses. You have to realise ice hockey coming here was a big deal. When they built the arena, drafted in all of these handsome Canadians and Americans to play in that first team, it was like a hurricane sweeping in through our town. It was dangerous and exciting and turned everything upside down. I needed something to cling to while my home life was in freefall. In the lead-up to their divorce my parents were constantly fighting and hockey became my escape.'

'Did I do something to hurt you? It was a difficult period for me. I wronged a lot of people and I'm doing my best to make it up.' There was genuine confusion creasing his brow into a frown but how could she clear this up without coming across as the pathetic, sad case she'd been?

'We only met in passing at fan events, signings and such. Nothing you'd remember.' Why should she, a gangly wallflower, have stuck out in his mind when there'd been so many confident, beautiful women tugging at his jersey?

'Sorry,' he said, the need to apologise for his past so deeply ingrained he wouldn't even know what he was saying it for.

Charlotte ached for the young boy who, like her, had probably grown up taking his parents' disinterest to heart, believing he'd been at fault. It put a different perspective on the rebellious player he'd been, whose misdemeanours now seemed so obviously a cry for help from someone suffering tremendous pain. His return here, facing up to those he'd hurt, had taken a lot of courage and she hadn't given him enough credit for it.

'It's not your fault. Really. I invested a lot in the team. Some might say too much. When you got tossed out of the championship match and we lost, I took it personally. A decade later and I guess I still couldn't shake off that disappointment when we were first introduced. I was afraid you might let us down again.' That wasn't half the story behind her initial resistance but it was the least humiliating half.

'It's understandable. I was a mixed-up kid and I let a lot of people down during that time. All I can do is apologise and hope you'll forgive me.' With that lopsided smile, that resignation as he accepted any blame that could be apportioned to him, it was impossible not to forgive him anything.

'I'll hold my hands up and say you're not the person I feared you were. I've seen what you've done for the team already, how you've handled Anderson and, of course, to-night when we fought to save Colton. There's no question of your commitment.'

'But there's obviously something else going on I don't know about when you keep running out on me.' He took her other hand, forced her to turn around in her seat to face him. Close enough for him to see through any lies.

She swallowed hard. This was where things got tricky. 'You were a big name in a small pond when you came here the first time. Exotic. Irresistible to a vulnerable teenage girl whose life seemed like it was falling apart. I might've developed a bit of a crush.'

That was putting it mildly but even that admission managed to raise his eyebrows and widen his grin.

He rested his hand on his heart. 'I'm flattered.'

'Don't get carried away. I *had* a crush. Past tense. There's no need to get all big-headed about it.' His ego didn't need to know adult Charlotte was beginning to develop more mature feelings on the subject. He'd probably worked that out for himself by now anyway.

'We never met or went on a date?'

'No. I just invested a lot of faith in you and let myself get carried away. I was genuinely devastated when you got thrown out of that game and we lost the championship.' With hindsight she was able to see that her lonely teen self had been dealing with so many intense emotions at the time she'd probably transferred some of that onto his shoulders, believing that he'd failed her too.

It was a relief knowing he didn't think she had a screw

loose, that he was on her side, but that didn't make the situation any easier for her to come to terms with.

'Do you see now why I gave you such a hard time in the beginning?'

'I do. All I can do is say sorry. Again.'

'I guess seeing you back here awakened all of those old feelings. It didn't help that I'd got it into my head you were hiding the real reason for your return. As I said, my issues.'

The colour slowly drained from his face. He edged back in his seat, regaining his personal space, and it was then she realised then she'd touched a nerve, that she might be on the verge of unravelling the truth behind his sudden reappearance. She instantly regretted this whole honesty thing. Whatever he was hiding, she had a feeling she wasn't going to like it.

Hunter was so overwhelmed with the information, so conflicted about how he should react, he was beginning to wish he'd waited until they were off the premises for the emotional edition of show and tell. If at all.

The line of this conversation deserved a dark, quiet corner somewhere with a stiff drink for both of them.

He hadn't suspected there was a history of anything other than his damaged reputation and it was almost worse, knowing the truth. It wasn't only the possibility of him failing her that had made her wary, it was the fact he already had. There was nothing he could do to rectify that except be honest about who he was now. He couldn't go on letting her think it was solely her paranoia keeping them from making any sort of commitment to each other.

That brought him right back to the subject he'd been avoiding. Alfie.

'I haven't told you the real reason I came back.'

She flinched, preparing herself for the worst and making him feel as though he was about to throw away that game all over again.

'I knew it.'

He could already see the barricades shutting down around her. Usually she had no problem telling him what she thought of him.

That defensive stance she'd taken instead might've been a better course of action for him than lashing out or self-medicating with alcohol. It could've saved his hockey career. Then again, it wasn't good to keep things bottled inside and isolate yourself, letting everything build up until some day it exploded and caused chaos, or slowly killed you from the inside out. He didn't want either for Charlotte, only for her to be happy.

'It's nothing bad. At least, I don't think so.'

Any earlier playfulness had vanished, any hint of a smile now evened out to a harsh thin line across her lips, and Hunter knew he should've found the courage to tell her about Alfie earlier. It didn't matter whether she minded if he was a father or not now, the damage had been done with the omission.

'I have a son, Alfie. I came back for him.'

He waited for a response but she said nothing.

'I didn't know he existed until a few months ago. My ex, Sara, was pregnant when I went back to Canada and didn't tell me. We all know what a mess I was back then so I can't blame her for not wanting me around. She died in a road accident last year and her parents got in touch. They thought Alfie should have one parent in his life at least. Although they aren't keen for me to have custody until they're one hundred percent sure it's best for him. Hence the move back to Northern Ireland and the need for a steady job.'

'I'm sorry to hear about Sara. I'm sure it all came as

a great shock to you.' The news he had a son had all but rendered her mute so she could only imagine how floored he'd been on finding out. It took any sort of relationship between them to a different level, one she wasn't sure she was ready for. Although Hunter hadn't been given a choice in the matter either by the sound of it.

He would have had every right to be angry about being denied the opportunity of that father role all this time only to have the responsibility dropped on him without a moment's notice. It showed the true strength of his character that he was trying to do the best thing for his son and put him first.

Discovering this new side of him had its pros and cons. It made her warm to him even more when the circumstances had just become even more complex.

'This was supposed to be a chance for me to make amends with all the people I hurt.'

'You seem to be doing pretty well with that as far as I can see.'

'I'm sorry I didn't tell you this up front but let's face it, we didn't exactly hit it off at the start. I understand why now, of course, but at the time there didn't seem the need to get involved in each other's personal lives.' He held his hands up but she knew that first day must have been akin to walking into the lions' den for him, with the lioness fiercely defending her territory.

'I understand.' She really did. If he'd announced he'd come back for his illegitimate son she probably would've imagined it was some sort of ploy to gain sympathy during those first days when she'd still believed the very worst about him. Actually spending time with him had taught her he was the new man he'd proclaimed to be after all.

'It's still early days for me and Alfie. I'm struggling to bond with him as it is without bringing someone else into his life. It was never my intention to get involved with any-one whilst I'm working towards gaining custody, and his trust. Despite the ridiculous urban myths, I'm not some sort of Lothario who'll welcome a string of *aunties* into his life.'

'No?'

'No. I'm deadly serious about all of my responsibilities these days.' He held eye contact with her until she saw the sincerity of his words reflected there.

She gave a tiny shiver, realising the significance of his decision to tell her about Alfie if he didn't invite just any-one into his son's life.

'It's my eternal shame Sara decided it was better to raise Alfie alone in secret than have his reckless, volatile father in his life. A decision I'm sure was very difficult for her to make and I don't want to hurt anyone to that extent again.'

'So, what's the problem between you and Alfie now? Is he having trouble coming to terms with having you in his life?' Charlotte understood that his ex had been trying to protect her son from the kind of questionable parenting she'd been subjected to but the very idea Hunter was con-sidering other people's feelings already made him a better father than hers had ever been.

'Quite the opposite. I think I'm a bit of a novelty given he's never had a father figure in his life before. Not some-thing I'm proud of and I desperately want to make up for lost time but I am a bit out of my depth. It's not helped by his overprotective grandparents who daren't let him out of their sight.'

'Okay, so he likes you, he wants to spend time with you… Surely they wouldn't mind if the two of you spent the afternoon together? Maybe somewhere local so they don't worry too much?' It wasn't fair that he should still be made to keep something of a distance when he genuinely wanted to be part of his child's life. She would've been devastated to find out her father had been kept from spending time with her. Unfortunately the opposite had been true for her. Her father had wanted to forget she'd ever been born so he could pretend he was still young, free and single.

'This is all new to me too. I'm not sure what kids' activities are age-appropriate for an eight-year-old. I don't have any experience of adventure playgrounds or family days out. At that age I was already practically living at the skating rink.'

'Can Alfie skate?' That sense of escape on the ice was something they definitely shared. As the son of a hockey player she would've imagined Alfie would've had that desire tenfold too.

'I don't think so. I don't know for sure. Sara wasn't into hockey and I doubt I did anything to persuade her otherwise.'

'Why don't you bring him to the rink? If he can't skate, I'm sure you could teach him. What eight-year-old boy wouldn't want to do that with his dad?' She put forward the suggestion with a shrug. It was all she'd ever wanted to do, with or without adult supervision.

'You're right. I'd have done anything to have had someone take me by the hand and lead me around the rink, showing some sort of affection, or even interest. Like all those other childhood skills, I taught myself how to do it because my parents hadn't had the time to spare. You know, I think they regretted my adoption because I got in the way of their self-indulgent lifestyle. They probably hadn't meant for me to be much more than a cute accessory, when I'd been a living, breathing little boy in desperate need of a loving home. That's why it's so important to me to get this right for Alfie.'

'I get it. We have neglectful fathers in common. Mine seemed to think divorcing my mum meant ending his relationship with me too. He threw nineteen years of marriage and family away for a fling with someone half his age. The one person I thought would always be there to protect me was the same person who broke my heart, and my mum's. I guess I was too much of a reminder of his failure as a so-called family man but he just walked away, leaving me confused about what I'd done wrong and why we weren't enough to make him happy. That betrayal of trust is hard to get past.'

'It is. I don't think I ever truly gave myself to Sara because I was always waiting for that final kick in the teeth. I needed to hold part of me back. Just in case.'

She nodded. 'I understand. I didn't even date until university because I was so cynical about the idea of love after the divorce. I missed out on those silly things young girls do at that age. There was no snogging in the back row of the cinema or hanging out in the local park in the dark for me because I didn't want to get close to anyone again. I couldn't go through that trauma a second time.' She shrugged. So much time had passed it shouldn't really hurt as much as it still did.

'See, this is why I want to be the best parent I can be for my son. I don't want to be the cause of him suffering that same uncertainty and fear. We need time together but just the two of us in the middle of that arena seems a bit intense. There's no distractions, you know, unlike the cinema or something. Maybe I should take him there instead then there's no pressure to talk. I don't even know if we've got anything in common other than our DNA.'

'You need to talk, to get to know each other the way we are.' She nudged his elbow to stop him fretting even more than he had been about the situation.

'It will help you bond much quicker than sitting in silence in a dark cinema. Listen, if it would help I could pop by and say hello, see how you're getting on. If all else fails we can break out a DVD at your place or something.'

Hunter was trying to do the right thing. All he needed was a little push in the right direction and if it meant one family could be saved some heartache she was happy to help. He deserved to have someone fighting in his corner and it might salve her conscience a fraction about her initial treatment of him.

'I'd really appreciate that, Charlotte. Exactly when did you get so good at dishing out advice to new fathers? Did you take a parenting class or something?'

She snorted at that. 'Definitely not. It's come from years of experience in how not to raise a child.'

'I'm sorry you had to go through it to be able to help me now but I am grateful to have a wingman for my first dad date with my son.'

'I'll pass on your thanks to the man who made it all possible if I ever see him again.' It was highly unlikely. Last she'd heard he'd started a new family and the last thing he'd want would be his adult daughter turning up and spoiling the doting dad illusion.

'So, as far as keeping secrets are concerned, am I forgiven?'

'You're forgiven.' How could he not be when he'd welcomed her into that sacred circle of trust?

This should've been the moment she'd wished him good luck and backed away. He and Alfie were a package deal and accepting that meant leaning towards the kind of commitment she'd always tried to avoid. She preferred her life uncomplicated but now there was a child involved it would change everything. She couldn't imagine the range of emotion he must've gone through on finding out he had an eight-year-old son he'd been denied all knowledge of but he'd accepted the role without blame or recriminations and had shown a maturity he'd been lacking during his last days here. Family hadn't worked out well for her in the past and this had bad idea written all over it. Except his determination to make a better life for his son made him the noble, loving sort of man she wanted to be around more.

All she could do was try and keep whatever emotional detachment she could from Hunter and Hunter junior and let them make that connection without becoming a part of it.

It was a long night waiting for news on Colton. Not to mention uncomfortable. Hunter had stretched his legs, making several trips to the vending machine for something calling itself coffee, and Charlotte had made several attempts to garner some information, to no avail. In the end the only way they were able to make themselves in any way comfortable was to lean their bodies against each other.

On a personal level they had taken baby steps forward but it would be inappropriate to take advantage of that when they were technically still on the clock and waiting for an update on their friend. That didn't mean it wasn't killing him, having her resting her head on his shoulder and not be able to pull her closer.

His cell buzzed in his pocket and he had to read the text from Gray twice before the contents sank in. He gave Charlotte a gentle shake.

'Hmm?' The sleepy response and the nuzzling further into his neck made a direct call to the side of him that had a tendency to forget the need for discretion.

'I've had a message from Gray. Look. We won.'

'What?' She blinked at the screen.

'They finished the match. We're in the finals.' He

couldn't quite believe it himself. The pride in the men who'd played out the game and won despite the awful circumstances swelled so deeply inside him he was fit to bust.

Charlotte stared at him then back at the screen and suddenly launched herself at him. Her arms wound around his neck in a tight hug.

'We're in the finals,' she said, and he couldn't help but laugh with sheer relief. It was the best news they'd heard all night.

'Dr Michaels? Sorry to keep you waiting but I just wanted to let you know Mr Colton is out of Theatre. The surgery went as well as we hoped for. We had to open up the thigh in order to operate so there is a significant wound that will be at risk of infection but he's out of immediate danger. We'll be keeping a close eye on him over the next forty-eight hours.' The surgeon who'd met them on admittance delivered another helping of good news with that same relieved grin he was sure they were all sporting.

'Can we see him?' Charlotte was wide awake now, on her feet, and would probably be in the room, checking on him, if she knew which ward he was on.

'He's sleeping now. I don't want to disturb him and it might be best if you change before you do see him.' There was a nod towards their crumpled attire and Hunter saw Charlotte tense next to him but it wasn't something she should take offence at.

'Of course. It wouldn't do much to aid his recovery to see us covered in his blood. Would it, Charlotte?'

He saw the penny drop as she gazed first at his crimson-stained shirt then her own. They'd scrubbed their hands clean since their arrival in the building but the evidence of the evening's battle for Colton's survival was in the very fabric of their clothes.

'No. It wouldn't be very nice to be reminded. We'll

come back in the morning to see how he is. Thank you for everything you've done tonight.' She shook hands with the man in green scrubs first and Hunter did the same.

'I think you two played a huge part here too. Now go get some rest.'

Hunter waited until the surgeon was out of sight before he took Charlotte's hand and marched her out of the building.

'What are you doing? Where are we going?' She was digging her heels in as they rounded the corner but they both needed to blow off some steam after the night they'd had.

'We need to celebrate. Do you really think the rest of the team aren't out partying now they know Colton's okay and they've bagged a place in the finals? We'll be lucky if they've recovered from their hangovers in time for the trip to Nottingham.'

'Look at the state of us.'

'It's getting dark. No one will see.' It was that time just before complete darkness moved in when everything was a muted shade of grey. The perfect camouflage for them to venture out in public without someone thinking they were two criminals escaping the scene of a brutal crime.

'Yeah, outdoors.' She didn't sound convinced but she followed him nonetheless.

That small sign of trust was a bigger prize to him than tonight's win over the Cobras. Now he was under pressure to produce something to deserve it. In the middle of nowhere. The gas station he'd set his sights on at the end of the road might not appear to be the ideal venue for first-class entertaining but he was determined to make this night memorable for the right reasons. He wanted to do something for her after she'd been there for him tonight, listening and advising on how to connect with his son.

'Wait here. I'll only be a few minutes.'

'What are you up to, Hunter?'

'Shopping,' he said vaguely, before leaving her on the other side of the automatic door. In truth he had no idea himself what he was doing but he'd improvise. They deserved some down time and a little fun following the stresses of the day. He for one wasn't ready to go home alone and attempt sleep when he knew his mind would be running over the alternative outcomes of their medical intervention and what could have happened out there on the ice.

Distraction filled two carrier bags and he hoped there was enough there to persuade his companion to remain in his company for a while longer.

'We all need to go through those silly teenage rites of passage and although there's no back row for us to mess around in, I'm sure I saw a forest park somewhere nearby.' He began his march again, thankful that the spring weather was being kind for once. It was mild enough for them to sit outdoors without hypothermia claiming them and that was unusual for this place. He'd been here when the first daffodils had been poking their heads through a layer of snow at this time of year. It was positively balmy here in comparison.

'Surely you're not being serious?' Her laugh rang through the darkness like musical wind chimes, bringing life to the still night.

He could just about make out the dull edges of the nearby picnic tables against the linear forms of the trees in the background.

'Always. Which is exactly why we both need a time out from being adults. I thought we could combine dinner, celebrating our win and Colton's recovery and pretend we're still teenagers all at the same time,' he said as he deposited his purchases on the wooden bench.

'In a picnic? Here? At this time of the night?' She wasn't more than a dark smudge now in the fading light but she did take her place at the table, waiting to see what he had planned. He had her engaged in something other than hockey or painful childhood memories at least.

'Never let it be said Hunter Torrance doesn't know how to party.' He unpacked a plaid travel rug he'd picked up at the cash register and laid it out.

'I don't think that was ever in doubt, was it?'

'Well, I've never done it *sober*. This was the closest I could get to alcohol.' He produced two small bottles of non-alcoholic sparkling white grape juice.

'I'm sure if I could see it I'd be impressed all the same.'

'Aha!' He rummaged in the bottom of the bag for the two glass candle holders and set one at either end of the bench before lighting them with the small box of matches he'd purchased too.

Charlotte sniffed the air. 'That smells very, uh, sweet.'

'Vanilla ice-cream, I think it said on the box.'

They flickered to life and cast a small pool of light over the scene. Charlotte's smiling face was revealed in the glow of the small flames and made all this effort worth it.

'It's making me hungry.'

'Good. Now, I'm afraid they didn't have a fine dining section because you know I would totally have shopped there. You'll just have to make do with chicken salad sandwiches and if you're good I might even let you have a cookie.'

There were many *oohs* and *aahs* as he laid out their makeshift dinner, both pretending this was some kind of grandiose feast. It could have been a three-course gourmet dinner as they wolfed it down with the same gusto.

'Do you woo all the ladies in your life with moonlit picnics in the park?' Charlotte surprised him with the question just as he was taking a mouthful of not-champagne fizz. Tears sprang to his eyes as he gulped it down the wrong way.

'I can honestly say this is another first. There have been no other picnics and very few ladies since Sara.' He couldn't even remember the last time he'd been this relaxed. These past years he'd been working his backside off, trying to rectify the mistakes he'd made, with no time for frivolity. Cutting loose with Charlotte showed him it didn't have to have negative connotations. The only thing that would make this perfect would be if Alfie was here too. It was all so easy when he was with Charlotte and he wished his rapport with his son could evolve as naturally too.

'Well, thank you. You've made me feel very special tonight.' She couldn't believe he had done this for her and had tried not to get too carried away with the romance if it was simply part of his usual seduction technique.

He'd come halfway across the world, given up his life there to come and be a proper father to Alfie, and she knew his son was his priority. Not that she would expect him to put someone he'd just met above that but they did seem to keep gravitating back towards one another.

'That's because you are. Didn't I say I'd share my cookies with you? I don't do that with just anyone.' He grinned and offered her the packet of chocolate-chip heaven.

She snacked on the crumbly biscuit and watched with fascination as he tidied the rubbish into the bin and laid the rug down on a patch of grass with the candles either side. 'Have I just sold my soul for a cookie? Is this where you sacrifice me to appease the hockey gods?'

'We could do that or, you know, just chill with some star-gazing.' He made himself as comfortable as he could, trying to fit his large frame onto half of the small rug, with his knees bent and his hands behind his head.

She had nothing to lose by joining him. Except perhaps all feeling in her backside when she tried to get up off the cold ground again.

'This is what you did as a teenager? I imagined something more rock and roll.'

'It might've involved a beer or two I'd sneaked out of the house but, yeah, I liked to lie in the quiet and just look at the stars. I used to imagine what was out there in the universe waiting for me, prayed there was more to life than the one I had.'

'You and me both.' Although she'd chosen hockey games as her fantasy landscape.

'Those three bright stars in a row are Orion's belt and that right there is the Big Dipper.' He pointed up at the constellation of seven stars.

'I think we call that The Plough over here but I've never taken much interest, to be honest.' There'd been nothing there to capture her imagination until tonight when Hunter had been so transfixed and the most relaxed she'd seen him to date. He looked just like the naïve kid they'd probably both been before real life had crept in and made them so jaded.

'I'm a bit of a nerd about it, I guess. I could bore you with the names of all those stars if I had a mind to but we're supposed to be having fun.'

'I *am* having fun. I didn't know you were into astronomy. I'm finding out so much about you tonight.' She knew every time she looked up at the sky from now on she'd always think of him and this night together. This gesture to recapture the childhood ripped from her was something she'd never forget.

He turned his head to look at her. 'Isn't that what you wanted?'

They were lying so close together she could see the twinkle in his eye. He hadn't planned this, she was pretty sure, but it had done the job. Hunter had told her everything she needed to know in order for her to let him into her heart. It didn't make it any less scary about taking that chance on him.

She reached across him so her face was only millimetres from his, her chest brushing against his, and watched his throat bob as he swallowed. As quick as a flash she grabbed the cookie from his hand and stole back to her own side of the blanket.

'This is what I wanted,' she said, and took a bite of her ill-gotten gains. It would do him good to be kept on his toes now she'd laid herself bare emotionally.

'Yeah? Are you sure that's all you have a craving for?' He rolled over and pinned her to the ground with one arm either side of her body and began kissing his way along her neck. It was so damn hot the much-sought-after cookie slid from her hand into the grass, now totally forgotten.

'Uh...maybe not.' She threaded her fingers through his hair as every blast of hot breath on her skin sent her into raptures. It was true. Ever since that first kiss she'd craved more of this, more of him, and tonight had taught her that life was so fragile you just had to grab the good times where you could.

'Good,' he murmured as he closed his mouth around hers and sealed her fate. She was lost to him now, whatever the consequences.

They ignored the first drops of rain as they fell, so wrapped up in each other they didn't care. Even when the candles fizzled out and Charlotte could feel the dampness on Hunter's skin she was reluctant to break away from him again. She was content where she was with his body pressed against hers and passion keeping them both warm. Unfortunately it couldn't keep them dry when the heavens opened and doused the flames.

She let out a shriek as they scrambled to their feet, the rain so heavy it was dripping off the ends of their noses and their clothes were sticking to their skin. It would've been romantic if not for the sudden drop in temperature and the very real possibility of pneumonia. They snatched up their waterlogged belongings and headed straight for shelter in the wooden hut where the forest route map was displayed.

'I'll phone for a taxi back to the arena so you can get your car.' Hunter wrapped her in the blanket, which was slightly less sodden than her clothes, and pulled out his phone.

Charlotte chattered her thanks through her teeth. As much as she didn't want this night to end, she needed a hot shower and a warm pair of pyjamas to get her body temperature back out of the danger zone. Sharing a bed naked with Hunter would undoubtedly have the same effect but sleeping with him wasn't going to make things any less complicated.

'I'd say that was a successful first date, wouldn't you?' Hunter tucked his phone back in his pocket and huddled in beside her.

'Is that what it was?'

'We're together outside of work commitments... Good food, great company... I'd call that a date.' He nodded his head, pretending that he'd planned the whole thing all along. If that had been the case he might've added an umbrella or a hot-water bottle to his purchases.

'You're a smooth operator, Mr Torrance, I'll give you that.' It had been her best first date ever.

A car approached from the main road and dazzled them in the headlights. Their ride back to reality.

'So, my place or yours?' Hunter leaned in and made her very tempted to carry on the impulsive nature of the evening but she was a woman who didn't give any part of herself so easily.

'It's a first date, isn't it? I'm afraid I'm just not that kind of girl.' She dropped a kiss on his cheek and walked non-chalantly towards the taxi, hoping their next dates would live up to the high standard of this one.

CHAPTER SIX

HUNTER WONDERED IF Charlotte might've had second thoughts about getting involved with a father and son when there was no sign of her at the rink. Now she'd had time to think about the implications of his tangled personal life there was a possibility she'd back out of the offer to support him today. They'd had fun in the park together but she hadn't signed on for a third party. Neither had he.

The strong connection he'd made with Charlotte hadn't figured in his plans when he'd moved out here but he couldn't imagine not having her in his life now. He didn't want anything to affect his relationship with Alfie but she was good for him and surely his happiness would filter through to his son too? A dad who'd found someone he enjoyed spending time with and could really talk with had to be better for him than a man still locked in his own world of guilt and regret.

His day was made with the sight of her walking in and giving him a tentative wave, as if she didn't really know if this was a good idea either. Hunter waved back, careful not to let go of Alfie as he took his first wobbly steps on the ice. This was an exercise in trust and if he let him fall it would be difficult to get him to have faith in him again.

He'd had to get Sara's parents to agree to this unsupervised afternoon out with Alfie and it did feel a little as though he was betraying their trust by inviting Charlotte along too. They hadn't been thrilled about the prospect of their grandson pulling on his first skates and Charlotte had been right about treading softly, not rushing things, when his relationship with the O'Reillys was still fragile, to say the least, but her presence meant a lot to him.

He tried to convince himself that this *chance* meeting wasn't deceiving anyone. It was more about having a friendly face around, someone to help fill the long silences with his son when he couldn't quite find the words himself. After their impromptu picnic in the park he was also happy to see her on a more personal level. He wanted that chance to reconnect and maybe even advance their relationship a little further too.

'I've got you. Don't worry.' He grabbed Alfie's arm to steady him as he began to lose his balance. One heavy fall could be all it took for him to lose interest in the idea of skating altogether and he wanted this to be the one thing he could do for his son that no one else could.

Alfie was still getting his bearings, clinging onto the barrier with one hand and Hunter with the other, as he tottered around the rink.

'Hi. I just thought I'd call in and let you know I've been up to the hospital to see Colton. He's doing well, all things considered, though he's not happy about missing Nottingham.' Charlotte skated out to meet them halfway around.

'That's good. I'll try and get up to see him myself at some point.' For some reason he felt as skittish as a boy on his first date. He was glad to hear his teammate was on the mend but he couldn't get past the worry over this meeting to truly relax. He'd spent more hours lying awake fretting over this than he'd ever had before a big game.

There weren't many women he imagined would've been willing to take on a hockey reject and his grieving son with such understanding. He was almost afraid to think his luck might be changing for the better since moving back here. Now he'd made amends for his past misdeeds perhaps karma had decided to give him a break after all.

'Hi!' Alfie too greeted her, giving Hunter the opening for an introduction.

To his credit, the boy wasn't shy about meeting new people, not even with the man who'd turned up after eight years, claiming to be his father.

'Alfie, this is Charlotte. She's the doctor for the Demons. Charlotte, this is Alfie, my son.' It still choked him up to say it out loud and held such significance the words deserved a choir of angels and light splitting the heavens to accompany them.

There was pride in being able to claim this beautiful boy as his own. The best thing he'd ever accomplished in his life was being his father, albeit a recent surprise. It also made him question his parents' behaviour more than ever. By blood, or through adoption, being a parent was a privilege, not a right, and those who'd professed to be his guardians had taken it for granted, abused that position.

After being declined the role and the chance of being there for Alfie's milestones, he couldn't imagine treating a child with the disdain he'd been subjected to. He hated all of those involved, or not, in his upbringing yet there was still a morsel of sympathy to be found in the situation. They'd never experienced the love and special bond between parent and child, and never would. More than that, they'd never know their grandson. He'd let them all know about Alfie's existence because there had been too many secrets to date but their selfishness would never let them accept another child into their lives. It was better for Alfie, and him, that it remain that way. He was just so afraid of making the same mistakes he was literally tongue-tied around him.

'Cool. Hi, Charlotte.' Alfie reached out to shake her hand and Hunter was pleasantly surprised that Sara and her parents had raised such a well-mannered young man. It made life easier for him and gave him more reason to be proud, even though he didn't deserve any credit for how he'd turned out. All he could do was continue to raise him in a manner of which Sara would've approved.

'Well, hello, Alfie.' Charlotte too appeared completely bowled over by his charm, which boded well for the afternoon ahead.

Hunter didn't know what he would've done if Alfie had blanked her or taken umbrage to her being here with them because he was sure as hell glad to have her here.

Unfortunately, Alfie's gesture left him off balance since he'd let go of the barrier. His blades slid from underneath him and Hunter had a job keeping him upright.

'Whoa, there.' Luckily Charlotte was there too to take his other arm and help steady him.

'I'm not very good at this.' Alfie's head went down and Hunter was afraid this wasn't as much fun for him as they'd both anticipated.

'It's all about balance. If you hold your arms out straight and bend your knees a little, you shouldn't need to hold onto anything.'

'Like this?' He recognised that stubborn tilt of the chin as his son gradually let go of his hand. That independent streak had definitely made its way into the next generation.

'You're a natural. Now just push off with one foot and follow it with the other. Good lad.' Hunter thought he would literally burst with pride at how quickly his boy was learning and following in his footsteps.

'I'm doing it!' The over-exuberance at his success set

Alfie off kilter again and the wobble was enough to bring Hunter and Charlotte back to catch hold of him again.

'This is your first time, right? Well, you're already doing better than I did. The first time I stepped onto the ice I ended up flat on my backside, with a bruise the size of a dinner plate.' Charlotte moved in before his confidence was too dented with one of her own painful tales.

'Well, they do say the most important thing to learn is how to fall properly. If you do feel yourself falling, bend your knees and sort of squat. Put your hands out to break your fall but make sure you clench your fingers into fists first.' He demonstrated the safest way to fall because it was a key part of the learning experience.

'Do you know something? I was able to skate by the end of that first lesson. All it takes is a bit of courage. Something I'm sure you have oodles of. Then someday you might even be able to play your dad at hockey.' She gave Hunter a wink and he almost lost his own footing. He'd been right to take her up on her offer today. If it was possible he could have both of these fantastic people in his life he would find a way to do it. As much as Alfie demanded he fulfil his responsibilities as a father, Charlotte was there to remind him he was still a man with his own wants and needs. He was able to be himself here today in their company, a whole person and not just someone playing the role he thought people wanted.

'And beat him?' Alfie's eyes were wide at the prospect, as if it was the coolest thing he'd ever heard.

'Probably.' Hunter wouldn't care. It would mean the world to him simply to be able to play hockey with his son.

'Can I try again on my own?'

'Sure.'

He happily stepped aside to let burgeoning confidence take flight, every shaky step bringing him closer to his son.

The three of them began to make their way slowly around the ice, he and Charlotte on standby to catch their student if he fell, but it wasn't long before Alfie was striking out on his own. Watching his son skate out onto centre ice could've been a scene straight out of Hunter's dreams about the future come true. A future which he was hoping Charlotte might become a part of.

He did what he always did to distract his mind and grabbed an abandoned stick left from practice and lined up an attempt on goal. There was nothing like smashing pucks into the net to prevent him from getting soppy about finding someone who really understood and accepted him, chequered history and all.

Before his stick made contact with the rubber disc, Charlotte appeared from nowhere with another hockey stick and intercepted the puck from him. She took off behind the net to slot in a wraparound goal herself.

'Easy,' she taunted, skating backwards down the ice, leaving him with his mouth hanging open and Alfie cheering.

'Where did you learn to skate like that?' He was impressed. She had proper hockey skills that went beyond the remit of the team doctor. Usually, all that was required for that position was an ability not to fall over if and when they attended casualties on the ice, and even then that was with assistance.

Just when he thought he knew everything about her, she went and surprised him again.

'I took some lessons when I was a teenager.' Things had been getting a bit too cosy for Charlotte, too much like a family day out, and she'd decided to break out a few of her moves to shake things up. She wanted Hunter and Alfie to bond but she was worried she was becoming too involved.

Goodness knew why she'd volunteered to crash this

father-son bonding session. It wasn't as if she had any more experience than Hunter did in these matters. She just knew by making the effort he was a good dad and she wanted to encourage the sort of relationship she'd always dreamed of with her own father. This waver in Hunter's confidence over his parenting made him all the more human and less of that two-dimensional pin-up on her wall with no real feelings or worth.

In the space of a few days he'd become so much more to so many people. The team needed him as their physio and friend, Alfie needed him as a father and, well, she just needed him. He'd invaded all areas of her life and suddenly she couldn't imagine not having him there to talk to, to have fun with, and to kiss when the urge took her. Yet meeting Alfie today represented a commitment of sorts on both sides and that terrified the hell out of her.

Today was simply about being emotional support for Hunter. By all accounts, it was the first time anyone had stepped up for him in that way. She was keen to make a good impression on Alfie too. The fact Hunter had kept him a secret told her exactly how much he meant to him.

She'd never contemplated having a child of her own, much less someone else's. That responsibility for another's well-being wasn't something she was prepared to take on when this thing with Hunter would probably fade before it got serious anyway. He had his son, she had her career, and those were totally conflicting priorities that could never gel long term.

No, she'd let this attraction play out until it became obvious they were still a world apart. That's why it was probably best for this informal meeting with Alfie here at the rink where there was no pressure. She didn't want him confused into thinking she was going to be a poten-tial mother figure. That would be too much, too soon, for all of them. He'd end up hating her before getting to know her if he thought she was staking a claim on his father when he'd only just found him. It was a minefield already.

With a flick of the wrist she scooped up another puck and tapped it from side to side, daring him to take it from her. Okay, she was showing off but she could see Alfie was enjoying the sparring. He'd even picked up a stick himself and she knew there was nothing father and son would love more than to face each other on the ice. Leaving her out of it.

Hunter suddenly set off down the ice towards her, and she gave an inward yelp whilst briefly thinking about making a run for it. Face on, he made an intimidating opponent, shoulders broad even without the padding of his kit, and thickly muscled thighs driving his every move. It was no wonder he'd struck fear into the opposition and love hearts into the eyes of his fans.

In this game you couldn't show any weakness, even when a powerhouse was headed straight for you. She stood her ground, hands clenched around the stick, bracing herself for the hit. At the last second before inevitable impact, he pivoted his hips and came to a slow stop, scooting ice over her skates.

'Just remember, us *brutes* have skills of our own,' he said, easily reclaiming the puck now she'd been rendered immobile.

Some men might have been miffed at getting challenged by a girl, many had in various aspects of her life when they'd underestimated her abilities. Not Hunter. That oh-so-kissable mouth was turned up at the corners as he squared up to her. Charlotte tried to come up with a smart comment to get him to back out of her personal space but he was so close, giving her that tachycardia-inducing smoulder, she could barely think straight.

'I think it's Alfie's turn to take a few shots.' She turned away from Hunter so she was no longer under his thrall. This exercise was supposed to cool things down, not turn her and the ice into a puddle with the heat they were generating.

'Sure.' Hunter adopted the goalie position, almost filling the net with his broad frame, whilst she skated back to find him a new challenger.

'I'm not sure I can...' Alfie was managing to balance with his stick resting on the ice but they all knew it would be a different story if he took a swing at a puck.

'Don't worry, I'll help you.' This was about him and his father having fun together and she wouldn't let this time end on anything but a high. She wanted him to make the memories she'd never had with her dad so he always had something to look back on fondly.

She skated behind Alfie and placed her hands either side of his waist. 'You keep your feet on the ice and I'll push. When we get close enough to the net you slide that puck in wherever you think you can get it past your dad.'

'Got it.' Alfie leaned over, knees bent and hockey stick in hand.

'We're coming for ya, Hunter!' she bellowed, getting caught up in Alfie's determination to show off his new skills.

'Bring it on.' The Demons' sexy substitute goalie grinned, urging his opponents to take their best shot.

She steered Alfie on a steady course to meet him and as soon as they reached the goal crease, he guided the puck to the tiny space uncovered to Hunter's left. Hunter stretched too late to prevent it from going in and Charlotte wasn't sure if she or Alfie cheered loudest.

In their race for a goal, no one managed to think about how they were going to stop and they collided with Hunter, all three tumbling into a heap. He took the brunt of the fall so they landed on top of him, laughing, in the back of the net.

'This is the best day ever!' Alfie took turns to hug them, the unsolicited affection taking her by surprise. She was like a rabbit in the headlights, unsure how to proceed for her own safety in case one wrong move spelled the end of life as she knew it. This was supposed to bring Hunter and his son closer, not pull her into the relationship. Yet she couldn't seem to help herself hugging him back, her heart melted by the gesture.

Hunter mouthed a *thank you* over the head of his son and she found she no longer noticed the cold seeping in through her clothes. The duo of Torrance smiles was more than enough to keep her warm. She was sure it was Hunter who'd become suddenly misty-eyed, not her, but the ball of emotion almost blocking her airway told a different story.

This was how a father was supposed to love his child and it highlighted even more what she'd missed out on all of these years. Parenting wasn't something that could be done from a distance. These two needed each other to feel complete and it was a revelation to someone who, up until now, had been content in her own company.

Family time was much more fun than she remembered.

Hunter couldn't remember his life ever being so full, or being so at ease with everything in it. It had been a busy few days and not solely because they were preparing for the play-offs. The afternoon he'd spent with Alfie had been such a success he'd been granted more access by the O'Reillys. It was all down to Charlotte. She'd had more faith in his abilities as a father than he'd had and simply having her there had helped put him at ease. That skating session had almost been like watching Alfie walk for the first time in hockey terms and as close to those missed milestones as he'd ever get. He'd be grateful to her for ever for facilitating that special day. It just wouldn't have been the same without her.

Since then he'd been able to pick his son up from school, take him out for pizza and generally do all the other things dads took for granted. As cautious as the O'Reillys were about his credentials as a reliable adult, he got the impression they were glad to have someone to share the childcare with and get some of their freedom back too.

The only downside of the whole situation was that he hadn't been able to spend as much time with Charlotte alone as he'd expected. It would be a balancing act of his time, trying to make sure neither was too freaked out by the other's presence in his life, but if Charlotte was going to be in his life she'd have to understand that Alfie came first. He was wary of letting things get too serious when he couldn't fully commit to her. Experience had taught him a very harsh lesson—a romantic relationship impacted on more than just him.

It was one thing to risk his heart again but he was a dad now. He'd hurt Sara by being so cavalier with her emotions and he wasn't about to do that to his son too. Unlike his parents, he cared about the damage he could inflict with a careless attitude towards his charge. He just hoped Charlotte was on board with his parenting approach too. Especially since he'd had to cancel their date tonight at short notice to babysit Alfie so the O'Reillys could visit a friend in hospital.

'Can we watch this one, Dad?' His companion for the evening selected a movie for them to watch together, a hugely popular animation that ordinarily would have seen him reaching for the remote control. Not tonight. He'd be content to sit on the couch with his son even if there was nothing but a blank screen in front of them.

'Anything you want, bud. Your choice.'

'Did you watch this when you were my age?' Alfie tilted his head to one side with that quizzical look Hunter had come to recognise. He'd become increasingly curious about his father's background, and whilst it was heart-warming that he had an interest in getting to know him better, Hunter didn't want him to delve too deeply. If possible, he'd prefer to avoid conversations about his family as long as possible.

'No. This wasn't out when I was a kid.'

'But you had cartoons in Canada, right?'

'Sure. Although the graphics are better these days.' And not the billion-dollar merchandise factory they were now. At least, he'd never had any expensive movie franchise toys but that could've been entirely down to his adoptive parents' refusal to spend that kind of money on a son they barely cared existed.

On the flip side, if he and Alfie enjoyed watching this together, Santa Claus would be raiding the workshop for every related item he could find this Christmas.

'Does it snow all the time in Canada? We only get it here sometimes and then the rain washes it away.'

'It depends on the time of year. We have seasons like everyone else.'

Alfie thought for a moment and Hunter was on tenter-hooks waiting to hear what would come out of his mouth next. The boy was clearly trying to process their different backgrounds and try to relate better to his father.

'Can we go someday? To Canada? Together?'

Hunter had been so consumed with getting his life set up here it had never occurred to him that Alfie might want to visit his homeland in return. It might be kind of cool to take him back, show him the sights and make some happier memories there. Some closure would be good.

'We'll have to talk to your grandparents about that but a vacation would be nice. Someday.' He wouldn't make any promises he couldn't keep but he would have the summer relatively free...

Alfie jumped up on the couch next to him, close enough for Hunter to know he was after something else. 'Maybe we could visit your mum and dad too? Do they know about me?'

They'd done it again. Somehow his parents still managed to ruin the good times without even trying.

'Yes, they know about you, Alfie, but I'm afraid I'm not really in contact with them any more. I'm sure we wouldn't find the time to see them anyway with all the cool things there are to do out there. You know Canada's the home of the Stanley Cup, the championship trophy for the winner of the NHL play-offs? I'd really love to take you to a hockey game over there if I could.' It was difficult to be diplomatic and avoid hurting Alfie's feelings at the same time. He could rage about his parents and what terrible people they were but there was no point in them being a black cloud in his son's life too.

'Oh. Okay.'

Not even the prospect of an NHL game was able to lift his spirits again and Hunter knew the kid just wanted to get to know his family. It was better for him in the end to keep his distance but he knew that heart-sinking realisation that wishing for something simply wasn't enough to make to happen.

'Don't worry. You've got me and your grandparents here to love you and we're not going anywhere.' He wrapped an arm around his son and gave him a reassuring hug. It was important in these circumstances that Alfie learned to focus on the positives, who and what he did have around him. It had taken years for Hunter to do that.

'And Charlotte?' Alfie looked up at him with hope in his eyes and Hunter was afraid he was going to have to disappoint him even more.

'Well, uh...' He didn't want to lie but neither did he know what the future held for him and Charlotte or how long she would be in their lives.

The doorbell rang and saved him from having to explain his complicated love life to an eight-year-old. He jumped up and practically sprinted to the front door to avoid that conversation.

'Hi, Charlotte.'

It had been Alfie's idea to invite her along too and Hunter had worried it was asking too much of her. Her last involvement with Alfie had been as a favour to him in an effort to get to know his son. A cosy family night in might be taking things too far, too quickly. Then he saw the bag of popcorn and the huge bar of chocolate in her hands and he realised she was in this with him.

'Are you sure this is okay? I mean, this is your time together. I wouldn't have come except he was so insistent on the phone...' She was already turning back before she'd given him the chance to invite her inside and he could see the debate going on in her head about whether or not this was a good idea.

The significance of her coming here tonight wasn't lost on either of them. She wanted to be part of this tonight, part of their lives and, regardless of the long-term implications, Hunter couldn't have wished for a better addition to the evening.

He threw the door open wide. 'Come in. You're more than welcome.'

The only thing that stopped Charlotte from throwing

the movie night treats at Hunter and beating a hasty retreat was the sound of Alfie laughing in the next room.
He was the reason she was there, gatecrashing their father-son time again, simply because she didn't want to let
him down. Hunter had been very apologetic with the last-
minute change of plans and his son's plea for her to come
over, and she had the impression he wasn't any more comfortable with the set-up than she was. It was natural for him
to protect Alfie by keeping her at a distance—after all,
she'd had the same worries about getting involved when
there was a child in the picture—but she and Alfie already seemed to have formed a bond of their own. Goodness knew, she'd missed seeing both of them these past
couple of days.

'Thanks. If I'd been left alone with all this junk food in
the house I might have been tempted to pig out.'

'I'm sure I can find someone to help you out with that.
I'll get a bowl.' He took the bag of popcorn from her,
leaned in close until his cheek was touching hers and whispered, 'I'm really glad you're here.'

With those words of acceptance she was able to walk
into the house knowing she'd made the right decision in
the end by taking the risk.

'Hey, Alfie.' She peeked into the living room to say
hello and make sure he was still on board with her being
there.

'Charlotte! Guess what? My dad's going to take me to
Canada and we're going to see someone called Stanley
and an ice hockey match.'

She needn't have worried as Alfie launched himself at
her, fit to bust with his news.

'Really? That sounds amazing.' Relations really had improved if they were thinking about taking an unsupervised
holiday and she was pleased they were getting on so well.

Hunter walked in armed with the sugary treats and rolled his eyes. 'Now, Alfie, what did I say?'

'Maybe. Someday,' he muttered into his shoes.

Those same words made Charlotte's stomach sink for him. She'd heard them over and over again when she'd asked her father if they could spend time together in the early days of her parents' separation. In his case they had always meant never but she knew Hunter was different. He was trying to build his relationship with his child, not walk away from it.

He set the snacks on the coffee table as he huffed out a breath. 'Well, I guess it won't hurt to price the flights in the meantime.'

His solid confirmation as one of the good guys immediately lifted the mood in the room and by the time the credits rolled and they'd scoffed their fill, Alfie was sound asleep in her lap and she was cuddled up against Hunter. The perfect night in.

'You two really seem to be hitting it off,' she whispered, so as not to wake the sleeping boy.

'You too. I'm really glad you came. The only reason I didn't suggest it myself was because I didn't think it would match up to the evening I'd originally planned for us.' He stroked her arm with the back of his hand, raising goosebumps with every stroke.

'Oh? And what did that include?' Whatever it was, it would be hard to top this right now, but he was being so playful it was impossible to resist finding out exactly what he'd had in mind.

'Dinner, music, a little wine…' His phone buzzed on the coffee table next to the empty popcorn bowl and robbed her from finding out what the rest of that evening entailed.

'I guess that means time's up?'

He nodded, already moving away from her. 'They're home from the hospital and keen to get Alfie to bed.'

'It's a shame they won't let him spend the night when he seems so at home here.' It seemed the most obvious thing in the world to someone on the outside, looking in, but she knew Hunter wouldn't do anything to rock the boat with Alfie's grandparents. He was being more patient than she would ever have expected given his strong emotions when it came to his son. During his playing days it would've taken a lot less for him to lash out and turn any precarious situation into complete chaos. She believed he'd changed from those days and she prayed Alfie's guardians would recognise it soon too.

He simply shrugged and gave a half-smile as he rose from his seat. 'Maybe. Someday.'

From him that was an optimistic outlook on what had to be an increasingly infuriating acquiescence to their wishes.

She eased Alfie's head onto a cushion so she was free again and reached for her shoes, which she'd kicked off at Hunter's request to make herself comfortable.

'What are you doing?' he demanded with a glare, arms folded across his chest.

'Getting ready to go home.' She was under no illusion she'd be part of Alfie's bedtime routine. It wouldn't do Hunter's cause any good if she rocked up at the O'Reillys' with the two of them. They were grieving for their daughter, about to hand over custody of their grandson, and she doubted having a strange woman on the scene would instil their confidence in Hunter any further.

'Is that what you want?' He was still frowning at her and for the life of her she couldn't figure out what she'd done wrong.

'I'm not going to insist on accompanying you back with Alfie, if that's what you mean. You can rest easy on that account. I'm done gatecrashing for the night.' She really didn't want him to be under the misapprehension she was going to wedge herself into both of their lives at every given opportunity. This was a one-off. Probably.

'That's not what I meant. I just thought you might wait here until I came back.'

Charlotte sank back into her seat. It might've been a swoon if she'd been standing up, like a regency heroine who'd been propositioned by an infamous rake.

'Oh? Now, why would I do that?' She couldn't help herself. Every time he alluded to spending some alone time she wanted him to spell out in graphic detail what he imagined that would include. It was as close as they got to dirty talk with a child in the room.

Hunter leaned down and whispered in her ear. 'I think we're past the dinner stage but there's always time for music, a little wine...'

In the end it was his unspoken intentions that had her bunching the upholstery in her hands as she fought arousal from completely taking control of her body. She was still sitting there, clutching the furniture, as he scooped Alfie up and took him home.

There was no mistaking what would happen if she waited for him to come back and she had to admit the idea of spending the rest of the night with him, in bed, sounded delicious. If it wasn't for the implications tomorrow morning. Then there would be no confusion about what was going on between her and Hunter. A few kisses here and there and they could still keep up the pretence there wasn't something serious going on that could alter the course of their lives.

Yet her feet still refused to move and her heart wouldn't quit yearning for the chance to truly be with him. Even for one night. It was a risk when every step forward with him brought her closer to that family commitment she didn't want, but tonight had shown her some risks were worth taking.

Not for the first time Hunter was glad he'd found a house close to Alfie. As much as he wanted to get back to Charlotte as quickly as possible, he was still able to take his time putting his son to bed. He was sure the grandparents hadn't approved of tonight's snack choices but he reckoned he had eight years of treats to make up to his son and a little junk food was fine in moderation. After all, someday these sorts of decisions would be entirely down to him. The consolation for their disapproval was Alfie's sleepy smile as he tucked the covers around him, which said he'd enjoyed the evening every bit as Hunter had.

Alfie had treated Charlotte more as a friend than a threat, or someone trying to replace his mother, and that was all he could ask for. In turn, she'd been her warm, kind, funny self and not once had she patronised or treated him with anything other than affection.

He hadn't even known he'd wanted her there until she'd been in front of him, but it meant everything to him that she'd wanted to spend time with them just for fun. There'd been no obligation, no plea from him to be a conversation starter this time, but she'd voluntarily pitched up to see them anyway. To him that proved she saw Alfie as more than an inconvenience or someone she was simply forced to endure. She genuinely cared. There weren't too many women who would've taken a last-minute date cancellation so well, never mind brought treats for her replacement. He was a lucky guy. One who desperately wanted to believe he could have it all.

The lights were still on in the cottage when he pulled up outside and he hoped that meant she was still inside, waiting for him. He hadn't planned any of tonight's events, they'd pretty much happened organically, but he did know he wanted to spend the rest of the night with Charlotte.

He let himself into the house to find her in the kitchen, pouring two glasses of wine. The hypnotic swing of her hips as she danced along to the radio drew him straight to her. Just like the earlier cosy family scene on the couch, it was too easy to forget this welcome-home sight was a one-off. But it was fun to play make believe every once in a while. He wrapped his arms around her waist and kissed the back of her neck.

'I found a bottle of white in your fridge. I hope that's all right?' She turned around to hand him a glass and took a sip from her own. He watched the liquid coat her lips and a sudden thirst came upon him that had nothing to do with alcohol.

'Was tonight that bad you couldn't wait for me to get back?' he teased, and took a sip before placing the glass back on the kitchen counter.

'I thought it would get the wine and music out of the way quicker so I could see what else you had planned.' She bit the inside of her cheek as she teased him right back.

He slowly and silently took the glass from her and set it down. Somewhere in the distance the saxophone sounds of nineties power ballads set the mood for seduction as he moved in. 'Nothing's planned. I thought we'd just see where the night takes us again.'

It took him straight to her parted lips to indulge in the tangy taste of wine and temptation. He inhaled the scent of her sweet perfume as he bunched her hair in his hands and deepened the kiss. She was most definitely real and his for as long as she wanted.

Over these past days she'd given him everything he could ever have asked for, joining forces to help him at work and at home, and trusting him not to let her down. That was a big deal given her past history and he wanted more than anything to prove he'd been worth the risk.

He cupped her breast through her grey sweater but the bulky fabric was too big a barrier between them for his liking. He loved her urban look, especially the tight black jeans that were showcasing her pert backside and long legs tonight, but the top layers left too much to the imagination.

'Take it off,' he demanded, his desire to see her, feel her turning his voice to a growl.

She leaned back and did as he asked, revealing a decidedly feminine silky black bra. He brushed his thumb over one nipple until it tented under the silk covering. Charlotte arched her back and primal instinct took over as he latched his mouth around the suckable point, taking fabric and all into his warm mouth. He flicked his tongue over the covered tip but it wasn't enough to satisfy either of them. He yanked the straps of her bra down her arms to free those perky nipples for his full attention. She fitted perfectly into the palms of his hands and he lapped his tongue over the soft mounds of flesh, lingering on the sensitive rosy peaks until her groans of pleasure were filling his head.

He skated his hand down her flat midriff, popped open the button on her jeans and made her gasp as he slowly unzipped her. Beneath her silky underwear he sought her moist heat with his fingers, sliding inside her so easily his breath caught in his throat. She was ready and waiting for him, yet he wanted to do this for her, give her some of the pleasure she'd already given him.

He made small lazy circles at first, opening her up to him, exploring her, with the slow, intimate rub. Those ever-increasing circles soon picked up pace to match her desire, stimulating that little nub of nerve endings that had his body at its mercy too. When he pushed his thumb into her she clutched at his shirt and he knew she was close. Her body tensed around him and his excitement reached critical levels right along with her.

She buried her face into his chest to muffle her groans, panting as he pushed deep inside her and that final burst of climax claimed her.

He was having trouble breathing himself and rested his head against her shoulder. 'Next time, I want to hear you scream, Charlotte.'

'Next time?' she said through hiccupping breaths as she adjusted her underwear.

'The night's still young and so are we.' Every muscle in his body was trembling with restraint but he didn't want this to be the end.

He took her by the hand and led her up to his bedroom, every creaking stair beneath their feet making this feel more illicit by the second when he'd never been more certain he wanted to be with someone in his life. This wasn't some random hook-up or a habit he'd simply fallen into and hadn't had the courage to break. He was emotionally involved with Charlotte and that made this virgin territory for him. Once he gave himself to her he knew there was no taking it back. It was a step into the unknown he was willing to take.

Charlotte's heart was about to force its way out of her ribcage if this man insisted on more of the same. This much arousal couldn't be good for a person. He'd brought her to orgasm without even getting naked and she was afraid once he did she'd end up needing a resus team. Not that it was stopping her from stepping into his bedroom. She'd always longed to see the wonders of the world.

She gave a shiver once the door closed and it wasn't only because she was still only half-dressed. Caught in the undercurrent of their passion, she walked towards him, being pulled ever deeper until she was in danger of drowning. Hunter undid the top buttons of his navy piqué shirt, which was stretched so tightly across his broad chest she couldn't wait for him to take it off. She lifted the hem and ensured he stripped off in double quick time to reveal a body that deserved its own social media account.

Sleeping with Hunter was a bigger event than she could ever imagine for who he was now, not who he *had* been. This wasn't about a teen fantasy come true, this was a real desire to be together, a connection between two adults who needed to get this attraction out of their system so they could get back to who they were outside it.

Okay, so she was trying to have her cake and eat it but she had a very sweet tooth and a libido that apparently wouldn't quit around him. Except every second she spent with him claimed a bigger piece of her heart with his name on it.

She mightn't be ready to be part of a family, or want to get hurt again, but it didn't mean she was made of stone. In these few moments of peace there was no talk of work, family or the future, only the silent acceptance of attraction. Here, away from the messy reality of getting involved, it seemed possible they could be together without causing some sort of cosmic fallout to rip the universe apart.

Watching each other undress was somehow as erotic as tearing their clothes off in haste. Perhaps it was because they never broke eye contact, the moment more significant than simply getting naked. They were stripping away the layers of their past, the outside influences they had no need for in the bedroom and concentrating on what it was they wanted here and now. Each other.

That didn't mean she couldn't see the impressive evidence of his arousal. It was difficult to miss.

She was only self-conscious about standing here stripped

bare before him for a few seconds because when he started kissing her she didn't care about anything else. He guided her towards the bed and she took him with her down onto the mattress, body to body, mouth to mouth, heart to heart.

With his finger and thumb he pinched her pebbled nipple and made her gasp with delight. Now he was aware that was her weak spot, he latched on tightly, sucking her into his mouth until she was bucking against him with unbridled lust.

She reached down and gripped his erection, sliding her hand along his shaft until she made him equally as breathless.

'As much as I don't want you to stop what you're doing, we need some protection.'

It was understandable he'd be more careful after having one unplanned pregnancy but she was restless against the sheets, waiting for him to grab the condom from his nightstand.

He lowered himself between her thighs and kissed her on the mouth as he joined his body to hers. Their breath mingled with a mutual gasp of relief now the veil had fallen. There was no more pretence that this wasn't what they'd been waiting for, regardless of all the obstacles in their way.

Charlotte hitched her knees up to her waist, drew him deeper inside and lost all inhibitions in favour of revisiting that place of utter bliss he'd taken her to earlier. She was close to the edge again already when she should have been exhausted after the last time, not coiled and waiting for more.

So far Hunter had been a gentleman. If that gentleman was a sexy stud acting out all of her very grown-up fantasies at once. She wanted him hard and fast, slow and steady, every which way he would oblige.

He filled her, stretched her with every stroke, and she rode with him, watching the intensity of the moment play across his features. The way he looked deep into her eyes every time he joined his body to hers, the breathy sound of her name as he buried his head in her neck and the tender kisses he placed on her skin said this was more than sex for him too.

If that was all this had ever been about they could have ended this in the kitchen or on the stairs, but he'd taken his time to make this right. It was as perfect as she could ever have hoped, except for one tiny flaw. She didn't want it to be over.

This feeling of completion was to be cherished, not thrown away because she was afraid of being hurt again. Regardless of the lectures to herself on the contrary, she'd fallen for him, again, and she wondered if she was hurting herself more by denying them a future together if there could be one waiting.

Hunter panted close to her ear and prevented her from over-thinking when it was far more enjoyable just to feel. She clenched her inner muscles as another wave of arousal crashed over her and clung tighter to him, her groans matching his as they reached breaking point together. Her cry filled the room as he fulfilled the promise to make her scream and she surrendered her body, her heart, once and for all.

After what they'd just shared it was going to be harder than ever to maintain that emotional distance she'd been clinging to desperately since he'd appeared in her life. She'd given him everything of herself now and she was trusting him not to fail her when she was taking the greatest risk of them all. Her heart.

CHAPTER SEVEN

HUNTER FOUGHT CONSCIOUSNESS because that meant leaving the warm, comfy confines of his bed and he wasn't ready to tear himself away just yet. He was happy where he was, thank you very much, with Charlotte's naked body draped across his, her hair splayed over his chest keeping him warm since the covers had hit the floor long ago. Probably some time in the early hours of the morning when his amorous companion had given him the best early-morning wake-up call he could ever remember.

If rendering him immobile with exhaustion was her ploy to keep him here as her sex slave he wouldn't have a problem with it.

Last night had been amazing on so many different levels. He was making such great progress with Alfie he'd been afraid to push for more time in case he upset Sara's parents, but Charlotte's support had given him the courage to move things forward and it was beginning to pay off. His dream of being a proper, twenty-four-hour father to Alfie was within reaching distance. What part in that picture Charlotte was going to play he wasn't certain but their time together recently had convinced him it could be a possibility.

'I suppose we should really get up,' Charlotte mumbled

into his chest, letting him know she was awake too and they had responsibilities other than their libidos.

He grunted his displeasure at the idea because talking took energy that could be better spent with one last period of play. Charlotte reached across him to turn the alarm clock around, her breasts squashing against him and re-awakening a certain part of his body.

He ran his hand over her pert backside, wondering if he could manoeuvre her into another performance of her cowgirl routine.

'I wanted to check in on Anderson today and see how things were between him and Maggie before he's shipped off to Nottingham.'

'You're thinking about another man already? You really are insatiable,' he teased. It was unsurprising she was starting the day with work at the forefront of her mind when she was so emotionally attached to the team. Her dedication was just one more thing to admire in her. Even if it did come at the cost of his comfort.

She smacked his chest. 'As much as I would love to lie here with you all day, we have jobs to do and people who need our help. You need to get up.'

'I'm nearly there,' he grumbled, knowing she was right even if his idea of how to spend these last moments alone sounded more fun.

'You can stay here if you want or meet me over at Anderson's in about an hour. I need to go home and get changed. It'll only cause a stir if I turn up in last night's clothes.'

Hunter watched with growing admiration as she walked around the room, still naked, collecting their discarded clothes from the floor. He propped himself up on his elbows to better enjoy the scenery.

'I think you missed something down here.'

His shirt, followed by his trousers, landed on his head, obscuring the view, but he could hear her tutting nearby.

'As soon as I put my mind to rest that everyone is match fit for the play-offs, I'm all yours. In the meantime, you need to be a big boy and get yourself dressed.'

'Spoilsport.' Though he hated to agree and deny himself these remaining moments with her, he had a few last-minute tasks to do himself, including saying goodbye to his son. Which he wasn't looking forward to. Even a couple of days apart was going to be quite a wrench for him.

By the time he'd taken his blindfold off, she'd wrapped the smooth curves of her body in the bulky quilt off the bed. Playtime was over.

He was aware her job and her reputation were everything to her but that didn't mean he'd go quietly. Sleeping together marked a change in their relationship and not something they should simply walk away from without acknowledging it. She clutched her quilted modesty tighter as he crossed the room towards her.

'I had a good time last night.'

'Me too.' She watched him through lowered lashes, surprisingly coy after everything they'd done together, to each other.

He wanted to tell her that he didn't want it to be over between them, that they should make a go of this, but those past mistakes haunted him still. Sara had had to deal with the mess he'd left behind for years and he didn't want to do the same thing to Charlotte if he wasn't one hundred per cent certain this was going to work out. The only definite commitment he was able to make was to his son.

'I guess we should face the outside world, though. I'll grab a shower and meet you at Anderson's. You can let yourself out, right?' He walked out of the bedroom towards the bathroom because he was having serious thoughts about throwing her over his shoulder and carrying her back to bed, pretending there was nothing to keep them from being together.

'Right. I'll see you there, then.'

Hunter didn't want to think about how small her voice seemed as he shut the bathroom door on her because he knew whatever happened next someone was bound to get hurt.

Charlotte was almost praying Hunter wouldn't be at Anderson's house as she walked the short distance from her place to his. It wasn't that she still wanted proof he didn't have her commitment to the job, she needed a time out when she could think clearly without their naked bodies getting involved. After last night she was risking her peace of mind more than ever by continuing to be with him. This wasn't just about him now, he came with an Alfie attachment, and she was fast falling for them both.

'Good morning, Dr Michaels.' Hunter joined her on the doorstep, waiting to be permitted entry to Anderson's personal life.

'Morning, Mr Torrance.' Pretending they hadn't just spent the last twelve hours naked together was going to be tough when her insides were already dancing with glee at the sound of his voice.

'Thank goodness you're here, Doc. There's something wrong with Maggie.' Anderson opened the door so quickly they were almost sucked inside by the vacuum he'd created.

'Where is she?' Charlotte pushed past him in search of the patient.

'On the couch. We were just talking and she collapsed.' Anderson and Hunter followed her into the living room where the red-headed Maggie was slumped in her chair.

Charlotte hunched down beside her as she started to come around. 'Maggie? My name's Charlotte. I'm a doctor. Gus said you aren't feeling too well.'

'Just a little woozy.'

Charlotte checked her pulse and felt her forehead but there were no obvious signs of anything serious.

Anderson appeared at her side, clutching at Maggie's hand. 'Is she okay? Is the baby going to be all right?'

'How far gone are you, Maggie?' There was already a small bump visible under her tight tank top but she wanted confirmation.

'Coming up on three months now but I only found out a few weeks ago.'

Which coincided with Anderson's descent into madness.

'How have you been feeling generally? Any nausea? Tiredness?'

Maggie nodded. 'Morning sickness, although it seems to go on for most of the day. I can't seem to keep anything down.'

'The first trimester is generally the hardest. It should start to get better from here on.' Not that she knew, or had ever intended to find out.

Hunter appeared at her side with a glass of water. 'I hear ginger biscuits can help with that.'

She couldn't help staring at him. That definitely wasn't information generally found in anatomy textbooks.

He shrugged. 'Internet forums. You know...'

She did know. Without a doubt he'd researched every aspect of parenthood the minute he'd found out about Alfie because that's the sort of man he was now. A wonderful, caring father who wouldn't leave anything to chance.

'I'll get some today,' Anderson assured Maggie, still refusing to let go of her hand. At least they appeared to have patched up their differences and that was good news for everyone.

'Have you had your scan yet?' It would probably put their minds at rest if they could see their baby was all right and might help Anderson get used to the idea of becoming a father. Make it real.

Maggie checked her watch. 'We were just on our way to the hospital for the appointment. We can still make it if we try.'

'You need to take it easy. Tell her, Doc.'

'Gus is right, you do need to take it easy, but I don't think there's anything serious going on. You're probably a little dehydrated. Make sure you mention everything at your appointment. You are going too, aren't you, Gus?' Charlotte would be happier if Maggie was checked over at the hospital where they could run any necessary tests to rule out anything more sinister and it would be better if Maggie had his support.

'I wouldn't miss it for the world.' He rested his hand protectively on Maggie's burgeoning bump, every inch the proud father-to-be.

Whatever had happened between the couple since Charlotte and Hunter's chat, he appeared to have grown up overnight and accepted his responsibilities. It seemed some men were capable of changing and maturing when they became family men, even if her father hadn't been one of them.

'I have to make another house call but I can give you a lift to the hospital if it would help? Trust me, you don't want to miss a minute of this pregnancy.' There was sadness in Hunter's voice and Charlotte knew all too well the reasons behind it. He'd been denied these early moments—the scans, the first kick and the anticipation of the birth. He was a good father and he deserved to have that chance all over again. That was exactly why this romance was never going to work long term. She wasn't the woman he needed to complete his family.

'That would be great, thanks. Are you okay to walk, sweetheart?' Gus was on his feet immediately, clearly keen to see his baby and get the all-clear as soon as possible.

She knew very well the difference a couple of days could make when it came to relationships when her uncomplicated singleton life now seemed a long way away.

'I'm fine.' Maggie smiled at him, the look of a woman in love that said they'd worked on those communication issues.

Hunter chivvied them all outside to his car. 'Are you coming too? I thought we could make that last house call together. We can both say goodbye before we leave for the play-offs.'

'If that's what you want...'

She knew exactly who and what he was talking about and damn if she wasn't a little choked up. It was a step further into his life, and into Alfie's, by taking her with him to say goodbye. That made this more than a casual affair. She knew he wouldn't risk hurting his son with such a move unless it really meant something and it suddenly made her want to take a step back.

Perhaps the intensity of last night had made her too carefree with her heart because now she felt as though she was standing on a trapdoor, just waiting for the drop to certain doom. She wasn't part of this family and that left even more chance she'd be the one left behind if things went wrong. As much as she wanted to be with Hunter, her self-preservation meant more.

They dropped Anderson and Maggie off at the hospital before they picked Alfie up for a spot of lunch since he was still on half-term holidays for school. If he hadn't already phoned ahead and told him they were coming, Charlotte would've backed out there and then.

She remained in the car at the O'Reillys' rather than cause any controversy by showing up on the doorstep and making any sort of claim on their grandson. In contrast, Alfie had bounced up as pleased as Punch to see her, and at any other time she would've been put at ease about joining them.

They called into the local fast-food place where the Torrance men devoured burgers the size of dinner plates before Hunter broached the subject of their trip.

'You know I have to go away for a few days?'

'With the team?' Alfie asked through a mouthful of fries.

'That's right. It's play-off season and we have to go to Nottingham for the weekend. I'll phone you every morning,' he promised, and Charlotte imagined it was as much for his own peace of mind as his son's.

Alfie paused in mid-chew and flicked a glance between Hunter and Charlotte before he swallowed. 'Is Charlotte going too?'

'Hmm-mmm.' She nodded then made a well-timed exit towards the bathroom, leaving Hunter to have that particularly delicate conversation with his son.

It was awkward on so many levels, not least because they hadn't discussed this weekend away as a couple. They'd be travelling for work purposes but it would be naïve for either of them to think things would remain strictly professional between them for the duration of the trip now. At best she was hoping they could have a what-happens-at-the-play-offs-stays-at-the-play-offs attitude to save her from getting involved any deeper and still get to enjoy the physical side. Not that they could explain that to an eight-year-old boy and she wasn't even going to attempt it. That was Hunter's call and nobody would thank her for interfering.

Unfortunately there was a queue for the one bathroom on the premises and she was forced to stand in the hallway around the corner, where she could hear the conversation she'd tried to avoid.

'She's the doctor for the team so, yes, she'll be travelling too.'

'Is she your girlfriend?'

Charlotte had to smile at the forthright Canadian side of the gene pool. Why dance around a subject you wanted a straight answer to?

'I guess... We've been spending a lot of time together. Would that be a problem?'

Alfie was worryingly silent, and Charlotte's heart was in her throat, waiting for the answer. It must be so much worse for Hunter. If his son didn't want her to be in their lives she knew he wouldn't force the issue, and where would that leave her? Time ticked by like treacle as they both waited for Alfie's verdict.

'I like her.'

'Me too.'

'Is she going to be my new mum?'

'I...er...it's too soon to be thinking about that. I don't know. Would you want her to be?'

'Well, she wouldn't be my *real* mum but she is cool.'

Charlotte's heart stuttered right along with Hunter's voice and she was unsure whether to duck back into the bathroom or leave the premises altogether. She couldn't breathe. The last thing she wanted was for Alfie to rely on her being around. The boy had only just found his father, found a stable influence, and it wasn't fair she should be included when she knew nothing of how to parent. She couldn't bear the pressure of that expectation if she and

Hunter didn't work out. Didn't want to be the cause of more pain and loss for him when she knew all too well how devastating that could be to a child.

There was no way she was lining herself up to be Alfie's mum, or anyone else's, and if that was what Hunter was looking for it was definitely time to back off. She'd already let herself get too involved, permitting her heart to take over from common sense.

Hunter and Alfie were still too raw to include her as anything but a passing acquaintance in their lives, even if they couldn't see it. If she was going to risk her heart and her dignity again, she needed some chance of a happy ending too. The wicked stepmother never got hers. It usually comprised a grisly death or a lifetime of misery.

She waited until they broke apart before she re-joined them. It would've been insensitive to interrupt them and immature to walk out without saying a word. In Alfie's eyes she didn't want to be anything more than a friend. A non-threatening, nothing-serious female friend. It was probably best if it stayed that way.

She plastered a big smile over her slowly breaking heart. 'Who wants some ice cream?'

It was her prerogative to eat her body weight in chocolate fudge ice cream to console herself when she was going to have to put a stop to this runaway affair.

'Me!' Hunter and Alfie chorused with their hands in the air.

She was honestly delighted for them that they'd built the foundation for a lovely life together. It just shouldn't include her in it.

By the time they'd polished off their desserts it was nearly curfew time for Hunter and Alfie. She'd seen him anxiously checking his watch, not wanting his allotted time with his son to end but unwilling to get on the wrong side of Alfie's gatekeepers. It was difficult for him and she wouldn't purposely make things any more complicated for either of them.

'Could you drop me home before you take Alfie back?' She ignored Hunter's startled reaction to her request, knowing full well he'd avoid a scene in front of Alfie by asking why.

In his head it probably made more sense for her to wait here or in his car until he'd dropped him off, so they could continue their quality time together. However, for her, that time had passed. If she made the decision to break up with him now before anything else happened it would be kinder in the long run. He got to keep his son and she got custody of her dignity.

They travelled the short distance back with Hunter quietly seething in the driver's seat next to her, hunched over the steering wheel, jaw clenched, forbidding a conversation he didn't want to have in front of his son.

'Thanks for lunch.' She was already unbuckling her seat belt and opening the car door before either of them had a chance to respond.

Unfortunately Hunter's quick reflexes hadn't waned since his hockey-playing days. She heard the engine being turned off and the car door open and close before she even had her house keys in her hand.

'Why the sudden rush to get away? I know I've been a bit preoccupied with Alfie but I promise I'll devote my full attention to you for the rest of the evening.' The growl in his voice and the sudden darkening in his eyes was promise enough of a good time.

Charlotte's libido insisted she abandon the moral high ground to taste the delights he was offering her. A night of passion from the man who could turn her insides to mush with innuendo alone was almost too hot to even contemplate. Every time he looked at her that way her body shivered in anticipation, but the fantasy was over.

'I would never deny you that time with your son. I know every second is precious after missing so much. That's why I'm taking a step back, Hunter. It's too much, too soon for me. I have enough to worry about with the play-offs. I'm sorry, this simply isn't going to work.'

There, she was letting him off the hook. He should be grateful she was making this easy for him, not frowning as though someone had confiscated his skates. Fatherhood had to be about more than his ego.

'I don't understand.'

He wouldn't because she wasn't going to tell him she'd overheard their heart to heart and make him feel any guiltier than he already did.

'Of course you're going to need to spend time with your son, it's only natural. What kind of person would I be if I didn't understand that? You two are making great progress and with Anderson back on track too we should probably quit while we're ahead. If you think about it, neither of us are in the right place to start anything just now.' She forced brightness into her eyes and smile to hide the shadow suddenly cast over her heart.

She was being honest in that she wouldn't deny them their time together—this was a child who needed his father, and vice versa. This situation simply highlighted the need for all the defence mechanisms she'd somehow forgotten in the chaos of getting to know them both.

It just proved how much you had to sacrifice for the greater good where kids were concerned, even when they weren't yours.

He stood there, forcing her to watch the pain and confusion burrow into his handsome features. So this was how it felt to hurt someone? How did her father or Hunter's parents ever live with themselves when her stomach was churning with self-loathing and a sudden urge to whip herself with birch branches?

'We've got the play-offs. We should concentrate on that and put this all behind us.'

'And you'll find that easy to do?'

'Yes.'

The intensity of his stare burning a hole into her soul, searching for the truth, made her breath catch on the lie. At least at the end of the season they'd be able to concentrate on their other priorities, away from each other.

'Right.'

It was a body-check to his ego but he'd get over it, over her, in no time at all. Really, they'd only known each other for a few short days. Not enough to expect him to spend the night crying wrapped in a comfy duvet, the way she'd probably spend her night. That was totally her prerogative. As was trying to be altruistic here.

'So I guess I'll see you at the airport.' She didn't hang around so she could feel any worse. This wasn't going to be a clean break when she'd be flying off soon for a weekend away with the very man she should be avoiding at all costs. There was a very strong chance she'd discover breaking up with him was the last thing she wanted to do.

CHAPTER EIGHT

ORDINARILY THE PLAY-OFFS were the high point of the season and this one should have been especially sweet for Hunter. He was back with the Demons and they'd made it to the finals. However, he seemed to have built an immunity to play-off fever. He was excited for the guys but it was no longer the most important thing in his life.

It had been harder than he'd imagined leaving Northern Ireland, leaving Alfie, even for a few days. He missed his son already. There was a hole in his chest, a void in his day and that awful sick feeling that something was missing. Not even his numerous phone calls home had helped improve his general mood.

In the end he'd had to concede it wasn't only his newly forged role of father that had him propping up the bar, staring into his drink, while the rest of the team was getting an early night.

He was missing Charlotte too. It didn't matter they'd shared the plane, the bus and the workload getting here, the emotional ties had disintegrated. Worse still, he didn't even know why it had happened or why it was bothering him so much.

He'd taken the grilling from the O'Reillys over Charlotte because naturally they'd wanted to know who she was. Regardless of the fact she'd cooled significantly towards him since their night together he'd defended his right to see her and had stood up to them when apparently having her in his, or Alfie's, life was no longer an issue. Somewhere deep down he'd believed Charlotte was worth taking the stand.

Ultimately it had been Alfie himself who'd put the argument to bed with a simple 'I like Charlotte. She's not my mum but she's Daddy's friend. And mine?' he'd added hopefully.

Hunter had nodded, only wishing Charlotte could've seen their situation in such simple terms too. He hadn't been actively searching for a mother for his son if that's what had scared her off. They'd been getting along well, so well perhaps he'd gotten too carried away with the idea of becoming a cosy threesome and she'd picked up on it. It was difficult not to let his hopes and dreams for the future shine through when he'd had everything he'd ever wanted as they'd skated around the rink hand in hand.

Charlotte would never take Sara's place in Hunter's heart because she'd given him Alfie but she did hold a much bigger part of it. Damn it if he hadn't gone and fallen for her. Now he was actually capable of loving himself and his son, it had left the door open for a wonderful woman just like her. Only her.

In trying to do right by everyone he'd messed everything up. He'd upset the O'Reillys and lost Charlotte, none of which was going to help his relationship with Alfie. This do-over had simply been a repeat of his past mistakes. Compounded this time because his son was old enough to witness his foul-ups and experience the consequences.

As he stared down at the murky depths of his pint he considered downing it and ordering some shots. A few years ago that's exactly how he would've coped with this— by blanking it all out so he didn't feel anything. Only the image of the disappointed faces of those close to him wouldn't let him flush everything he'd worked so hard for down the toilet. He'd done that once before and it had been too damned hard to get back to where he was now to go down that same dead end.

'Hunter Torrance. I'd heard you were back in town.'

He almost had the self-pity knocked out of him as a meaty palm slapped him squarely between the shoulder blades. His hand clenched in a fist in an automatic response and released again when he saw who it was. Chris Cooper, CC to his teammates, had spent a couple of seasons at the Demons before he'd moved to England to play.

Now he was assured it wasn't someone here in Nottingham wanting to settle an old score, Hunter happily shook hands and ordered his old friend a drink.

'Yeah. I'm the physio for the Demons these days.'

'I'd heard that.' CC nodded sympathetically, as many did on hearing about the career change. It didn't bother Hunter any more.

'And you? Still involved in the game?' He hadn't kept in touch with anyone, too busy trying to sort his own life out to keep track of anyone else's.

'You could say that.' CC grinned and took a mouthful of lager.

Hunter did the same, his mouth suddenly dry with that awful sensation he'd missed something big. Most of the guys he'd played alongside were retired these days and he hadn't seen any familiar names on the coach roster apart from Gray. That only left 'Management?'

'I made a few property investments along the way, made my name there after I retired and was able to buy my way back into the game. I'm part owner of the London Lasers now.' There was no boasting there, more of an I-know-I'm-a-lucky-son-of-a-gun vibe from him, but to have that sort of clout in the industry took more than a well-timed gamble.

'Impressive. So I take it you're settled in London, then? Wife? Kids?' CC had been a blow-in, just like him, so there would've been some reason for him to stick around after his playing days were over. Perhaps if Hunter had known about Alfie he wouldn't have left either.

'Married to Lenora for five years and we have two girls, Lily and Daisy.' He was beaming now, his already ruddy complexion shining with pride, and Hunter was alarmed to find he envied his marital status more than his bank balance.

Precisely when had he become the settling-down type, yearning for a wife and two point four children? Probably around the time Alfie and Charlotte had crashed into his life and turned it inside out. He'd had his days of partying and reckless behaviour. Now he found more pleasure in simply being in the company of those he loved. He didn't have to chase the good times any more when they came so easily. At least they had done until recently. He took another gulp of beer.

'What about you? Who, or what, brought you back?'

It was a simple question, an obvious one between two old friends catching up, yet Hunter took his time replying. His circumstances weren't wrapped up as succinctly as his new drinking buddy's but he was done with keeping secrets.

'I have a son, Alfie. Things didn't work out between me and his mum. As I'm sure you're aware, I…er…had a few problems back in the day.'

'Kudos to you for getting back on your feet.' CC held his glass up to toast him before a split second of panic hit. 'This is okay, isn't it? I mean, I'm not enabling your fall off the wagon here or anything?'

That was always going to be a worry for everyone who'd witnessed his overindulgence, and something he made sure to keep in check himself, but he wasn't that same hurting, out-of-control kid any more.

He clinked his glass to CC's. 'Those days are long gone. I'll be tucked up in bed after this one. I've turned into something of a bore since becoming a dad.'

'Some might call it being responsible. There's nothing like having kids to curtail the partying. So, you're settled for good in Ireland?'

'That's where Alfie is.' He'd never really considered being anywhere else.

'And you have a permanent position with the Demons? It's all set in stone?' CC was digging even deeper than Charlotte had in the beginning but Hunter had no more skeletons lurking in his closet. At least, none he was aware of.

'Well, no. Not as yet. I was drafted in on a handshake. I'd like to stay on but I'll be working on building up my own practice too once I'm settled.' That had been his original plan but reaching out to Gray had given him his lucky break and enabled him to make the move sooner than expected. It might've been a trial run but it was also a pay cheque whilst he got to know his son.

'Hmm.' CC twirled the cardboard beer mat between his fingers, his mind working overtime somewhere else.

'Hmm, what?'

'We could do with a stand-up guy like you with the Lasers. We've built up quite a medical team focused on strengthening our players. It would be good to have you on board next season.' The steely set of his jaw said this was a serious offer, not a throw-away comment over drinks.

'Are you serious? I mean, the last time we saw each other I was a bit worse for wear.' Whilst the job offer had damn near knocked him off his bar stool, he didn't want CC to be mixing him up with someone else.

'I think tossing the entire team's collection of sticks across the ice was a particular highlight but, yes, I'm serious.' He rested his elbow on the bar top and leaned in. 'Look, everyone deserves a second chance. I've been there myself. Let's just say there was a dark period in between hockey and the property empire. I know what it takes to start over and that's the kind of strength and determination I like to see on a résumé. Besides, who's in a better position to know what hockey players' bodies go through than an ex-pro?'

This had come so out of the blue Hunter couldn't process it and found himself having to break it down in simple terms to get his head around it. 'You're *actually* offering me a job? In London? Wow!'

CC nodded and his belief in Hunter's abilities on face value made it tempting to latch onto the exciting opportunity. A job in London could set him up financially for some time to come and offer so many opportunities for him and Alfie. A new city, new team might finally help him put the past behind him for good. He'd only been in the dad role for a short time and he'd already fallen back into old habits by getting involved with someone without properly thinking it through. He still had to find a way to break it to Alfie that Charlotte would no longer be in their lives and the last thing he wanted to do was let his son get hurt in the crossfire of his love life.

A new start away from the everyday reminders of his failures might be just what they needed to start healing. It wouldn't hurt to find out a bit more about it at least.

'Come see me tomorrow before the game. We can have a proper discussion in private.' CC pulled a business card from his wallet and gave it to Hunter.

CC downed his pint and shook Hunter's hand as he got up to leave. 'Oh, and good luck for the finals. You're gonna need it.' Even here and now between old teammates the competitive spirit was alive and kicking.

'We don't need luck when we've got skills, bro.' Hunter popped the sophisticated silver and black calling card into the back of his wallet along with the picture of his son.

As he'd discovered, life never panned out the way he often expected and he had to make the most of opportunities like this where he could. It wasn't every day he found people who still had faith in him. Charlotte had been the first person in a very long time to show that belief in him as a father and a medical professional and he'd lost her. Perhaps it was time to start over with a clean slate somewhere new.

The atmosphere between Charlotte and Hunter since that afternoon with Alfie felt as though someone had run the Zamboni right through it, coating the surface with fresh ice. It seemed to her they were both afraid to take the first step out and be responsible for leaving deep grooves in the calm, crisp surface.

Things had been as cool as could be since they'd boarded the plane to Nottingham. They hadn't moved on from small talk about the team injury list. It was probably for the best. If they ventured into more personal matters she might actually break and tell him she'd overheard his conversation with Alfie and panicked and she didn't want him to talk her around, tell her things would work out. She was getting in way too deep.

Hunter Torrance, her colleague as well as a single father, was more heartbreak waiting to happen. More than she was going through now. She could just about bear the broken glass stabbing pain in her chest every time she saw him, every time she imagined his lips on hers. Another afternoon spent playing happy families only to have it torn apart again would shatter what was left of her soul.

If she'd let herself get drawn any further into their developing relationship it would've meant opening her heart up for two, double the potential sense of loss when it didn't work out. It couldn't work out. Hunter was a family man now and she was a career woman. One successful season with the Demons and her client list would be a mile long at her own clinic. Her job was her baby and it wouldn't hurt anyone but her if she failed at it. Not that she had any intention of that now it would be receiving her full attention again.

'Anderson certainly seems to be back on form. He showed me the baby scan. I guess fatherhood really does change a man.' Even with the sound of the crowd ringing in her ears she couldn't bear the silence between her and Hunter as they stood and watched the game, or the noise of her own thoughts.

The Demons had five minutes left in the third and final period of play in their match with the Glasgow Braves. They were one nil down and to her amazement Anderson hadn't lost his cool once, even after a dodgy offside decision. He'd taken it on the chin and got straight back into the game without wasting a second of play. A week ago he'd probably have been in danger of being prosecuted for GBH.

'Maggie's here, supporting him, and I know they've told their folks about the baby so I guess it all worked out. It's amazing what simple communication can do for a couple.' The barbed comment said he was still miffed by the way she'd ended things.

Okay, she mightn't have handled it perfectly but she'd been in a panic. She didn't respond well when cornered and that's how she'd felt, trapped, listening to his heart to heart with his son. Over these past years she'd learned to run rather than walk away when things started to get serious and they didn't get more serious than having a kid in the picture.

'Hunter, I—' Her lame apology and explanation was cut off by a deafening cheer as Anderson scored an unassisted goal.

He didn't hear her attempt to build bridges, celebrating the equaliser with his own 'Yes!' as he punched the air.

That unexpected surge of vocal passion gave her chills beneath her fleecy jacket, pinching her nipples into little beads of need begging to experience that passion again for herself.

She would've failed to snag his interest again even if she had figured out what to say as tempers began to fray on the ice. With everything to lose in this semi-final both teams were involved in a bit of pushing and shoving, trying to reclaim possession of the puck. One of the Glasgow players received a two-minute penalty for roughing, giving the Demons a power play, an extra man on the ice, in the dying moments of the game.

Shot after shot was launched at the opposition's net with the one-player advantage, each successfully blocked by the net minder as the seconds ticked down on the scoreboard,

Ten. Nine. Eight...

The sound of sticks hitting rubber echoed around the arena as players valiantly fought for victory and fans held their breath for that last burst of emotion, be it joy or sorrow.

Time seemed to stand still, players moving in slow motion as they made their final attack. The battery of Demons launched themselves down the ice in a fearsome display of gladiatorial determination to survive the battle.

Seven. Six. Five...

The puck passed from player to player, taking the game towards the opposition. Both teams crowded into the penalty area, a scrum ensuing in the goalmouth. The Demons' captain, Floret, claimed the last shot with a mighty thwack.

Goal!

The Demons were play-off finalists.

The arena erupted and as ecstatic as Charlotte was about the win, she knew she and Hunter wouldn't have a chance to reconnect for the rest of the evening. Tonight's success and preparation for tomorrow's battle would keep them otherwise engaged. She should've been glad there was less chance she'd have to explore that idea of communication he was keen on but tomorrow officially ended the season, and with it this period of her life with Hunter. Even if they both returned next season, this break sounded the death knell of their relationship.

Instead of making her feel light and carefree, the thought of no longer being part of Hunter's or Alfie's lives left her feeling numb.

It was difficult to get the players to sit still long enough for a post-game check-up. They were still buzzing behind the scenes long after that final klaxon sounded their win.

'You need that hand seen to.' She practically had to drag Evenshaw into the room so she could treat him.

'Don't fuss. It's only a scratch,' he said, wiping the blood down his shorts.

Men, why did they have to be so damn stubborn?

Take Hunter, for example. She'd ended their relationship and yet he wouldn't stop staring at her as if he had a right to.

As the visiting side at the arena, they didn't have the luxury of the space they had at home to treat their patients. She was currently sharing the small box room with Hunter, acutely aware of his eyes on her regardless of the sweaty players swarming in and out.

With an antiseptic wipe she cleaned the blood away from her patient's palm and watched him wince despite his protestations anything was wrong. It was a clean slice, probably from someone's blade, which thankfully wasn't too deep. She'd seen a lot worse recently. It was a sport where speed, sharp skates and rivalry definitely didn't mix well.

'You'll be pleased to know you don't need stitches.'

'See. I told you.' He attempted to get up to join the rowdy celebrations next door.

'Sit.' She pushed him back down into the chair so she could dress the wound properly.

'Yes, ma'am! I do like a woman in charge.' His tooth-less grin and flirty wink got him nothing except a cuff on the shoulder.

It was a joke, something she didn't take too seriously, but one look at Hunter and she was worried he might wade in and try to protect her honour.

'Ouch. Not so hard.' The unfortunate player on the massage table took the brunt of his apparent rage. Some might have said kneading muscles a tad too roughly was an improvement on smashing up equipment but Charlotte doubted his current patient would agree.

'Sorry.' Hunter returned his gaze from Charlotte back to the burly thighs of the net-minder who'd overstretched during his heroic saves.

'So...can I go now?' Her patient's impatience drew Hunter's attention once more.

'Er...yes. Try to keep that dressing dry and stay away from sharp objects.'

'Yes, ma'am.' He didn't need to be told twice and bolted towards the ruckus going on in the locker room.

'You're finished too.' Hunter gave his permission for the net-minder to go and join the celebrations too as he went to wash his hands.

Within seconds Charlotte and Hunter were alone for the first time since she'd called things off and she tried to get out as quickly as possible to avoid a scene.

'I'm looking forward to the team dinner. It's the most important meal for staff as well as players. I think we all need to replenish our energy stores with protein and slow-acting carbs. I'm starving.' It was a lie. Food was the last thing on her mind but if they were going to have to talk she wanted to keep it neutral.

'What happened to us, Charlotte?' Hunter seemed to see straight through her bluster, his calm, measured voice a contrast to her erratic rambling. It made her question who was actually having more trouble accepting the break-up.

'It doesn't matter, it's over.'

'Just tell me why and I'll walk away. I won't bother you again.'

She knew she couldn't keep lying to him because he'd torture himself about what he'd done wrong when in truth he'd only ever done right by his son.

'I overheard you and Alfie talking and I… I couldn't have him thinking that I'm going to be part of this new life you have planned together. It would only end in tears. His and mine if we'd carried on believing in the fairy-tale. I'm sorry.'

He stared at her, unblinking, probably trying to rewind back to that supposedly private conversation. 'Charlotte, he's a frightened eight-year-old boy still mourning the loss of his mother. You think I should've put him right and said we're just having a fling? I was trying to protect his feelings, to reassure him there isn't going to be any more disruption in his life. I wasn't asking you to be his replacement mother. All I wanted was for you to give us a chance. I'm trying to be careful about saying and doing the right thing so I don't hurt anyone again the way I did his mother.' Hunter's sincerity climbed along the back of her neck and stood the hairs there to attention.

'I guess it doesn't matter now.' If only they'd managed to leave emotions other than rampant lust out of the equation she might still be with him. Except she knew her feelings for him had gone way past merely the physical aspects of being together and distance was no longer a safety net for her fragile heart.

'I guess not.'

'We'll chalk it up as another one of those teenage impulses we needed to get out of our system.' She forced a smile but she felt sick to the stomach pretending that was all it had been to her, and to him. A part of her wanted him to fight for her and salvage something of what they'd had but he remained silent, unmoved by the suggestion.

There was a sharp knock on the door, calling time on their heated confessional. 'Let's go, people. The party bus is here.'

'We should really try and catch up with everyone before they leave without us.' She turned towards the door, unable to look at him any more without tears filling her eyes. It really was over.

Hunter needed to go along with Charlotte's decision to end things because it had become impossible to ignore the growing feelings he had for her. She was much more than a friend to him. Generally, his buddies were a lot hairier, missing a few teeth, and only good company over a beer or two. He didn't spend every waking moment thinking about kissing them or wanting to knock out one of their players for coming onto her.

After everything she'd told him about her past he could see why she was wary about getting too close but that chemistry between them wouldn't simply dissipate because they deemed it inconvenient. It made London seem more appealing by the second if Charlotte was never going to be part of the family he wanted for himself and Alfie. He couldn't see her day after day at work, pining for her yet knowing she didn't feel about him the way he did about her. She was right—it wasn't fair for Alfie either to watch him develop an attachment to someone who wasn't in this for the long haul. There didn't seem any point in fighting for someone who clearly didn't want them in her life.

They made their way back out the maze of corridors to find the team bus but a familiar meaty hand on his back soon stopped him in his steps.

'Good game, eh? I suppose it doesn't matter to you who wins or loses now. After today I do expect your loyalties to lie with the Lasers. Glad to have you on board, bud.' Another back-slap Hunter could've done without forced a strained smile on his face. CC wasn't to know his timing was completely off. It was no one else's fault but his own that he hadn't mentioned their conversation with Charlotte yet.

'What's he talking about?' She was staring at him, not seeing CC's departure, only his revelation.

'I've been offered a permanent position with the Lasers.'

'You're leaving?' Her brow knitted into an ever-deepening wound.

'I agreed to a meeting. That's all.'

'What about Alfie?'

'It was Alfie I was thinking about when I said I might be interested. I thought it could be a new start for both of us in London.'

'What about the team?'

'It was only meant to be a temporary position. I'm sure Gray would understand if it came down to it.'

'What about me?' Her voice was small, almost impossible to hear even in the relative quiet of the arena as the Zamboni trundled out to begin cleaning the ice. If only life was as easy to start afresh, leaving no trace of past traumas, people would be a lot happier with their lot.

'You said you didn't want to be part of us.' Yet he could see the hurt etched in her furrowed brow and her soulful brown eyes.

'So the first sign of trouble and you're running away again? I thought you were the kind of man who fought for the things that mattered? I guess that really doesn't include me.' She folded her arms across her chest as if she was protecting her heart. He knew his was breaking with every painful second he spent with her, unable to touch her or tell her how he really felt about her because there was no room for second thoughts when it came to Alfie's future.

'I'm not running from anything. You were the one who didn't want commitment, remember? I was just—'

'Keeping your options open? I said I didn't want to commit to you and Alfie because I was afraid I'd get hurt. Turned out I was right all along. There is no room for me in your life. Not really. I'll always be the one you leave behind if a better offer comes along.'

'I'm a washed-up hockey player in the back of beyond. Of course I'm going to jump at the chance of a better life for my boy. He is always going to come first.' He couldn't care less about the money or social status, that stuff had stopped being important a long time ago. The truth was, the idea of him, Alfie and Charlotte cosied up in his cottage would be bliss if it were possible. Recent events had shown him it wasn't. It was selfish of him to have believed he could have everything he wanted, someone was always going to suffer as a result.

Ten years ago this would've been much easier. That cavalier attitude to other people's feelings wouldn't have given him this stabbing pain in his gut. At times such as this he missed the old Hunter who hadn't cared about anything except making time to wallow in liquor or his own self-pity.

'Of course he is. Well, good luck in London, then.' Charlotte turned her back on him and walked away, her refusal to lose her cool and get emotional harder to watch than if she'd burst into tears. It signalled her retreat back to where she'd been when they'd first met. She'd been right in trying to protect herself from him all along. He was still making those same mistakes, hurting people he loved and walking away from the devastation.

This was the last time and it was for the right reasons. From now on he was completely devoted to Alfie. As he should've been from the start.

CHAPTER NINE

DINNER HAD BEEN an awkward affair. At least between him and Charlotte. Much like having to live under the same roof after a break-up. An impossible situation that couldn't be avoided and made for a very frosty atmosphere. It wasn't helped now they were back on the team coach on the way back to the hotel with darkness falling outside. She'd taken the aisle seat across from his rather than the empty one beside him. Close enough to prevent any questions being asked about why they were avoiding each other but also putting that significant distance between them. If there'd been no other available seats it wouldn't have come as a surprise if she'd chosen to sit on the floor rather than next to him again.

He didn't blame her. All he'd done lately was confirm both of their fears he would always be the same flaky guy he'd always been, no matter how hard he tried.

'Right, guys. Can I have your attention front and centre, please?' Gray stood at the front of the coach, clapping his hands for attention, diverting it from poker games, cellphones or the very attractive team doctor.

The bus lurched over a pothole, jogging everyone in their seats except Gray, who was undeterred from his motivational speech at the front. He simply planted his feet on either side of the aisle and gripped the headrests of the front seats. 'I know I've already said it—'

'Yeah. Probably at the last speech you gave about ten minutes ago.' The brave heckler at the back prompted a chorus of whoops and whistles.

Gray raised his hand to calm the noise back to an acceptable level. One where his voice was the only one getting airtime.

'Let's not get too cocky. As I was going to say, congratulations on tonight's win. You deserved it and I know we were all thinking of Colton out there.' He started a round of applause for the performance, which Hunter and Charlotte enthusiastically joined.

Getting to the final was a big deal. The season tended to be pretty flat if it ended before they made it to Nottingham so the fact they'd made it all this way had left most of them on a high. With any luck they'd be taking the trip back home with some silverware so they didn't have to come back down to earth too soon.

Gray motioned for silence again. 'That being said…'

There was a collective groan as they waited for the kicker.

'Tomorrow is another day, another game, and there's no time for resting on our laurels. I want you all up bright and early for drill practice.'

Another groan went up. Although Gray didn't linger on sentiment too long, pride was there in his grin. Somehow he managed to make Hunter feel a part of it all. That sense of belonging was something he'd been searching for a long time but he was afraid to embrace it. Nothing in his life had ever been secure for long and he wanted to change that for Alfie as well as himself.

Suddenly, there was a loud bang, followed by the

screech of tyres as the bus jolted from side to side and the driver tried to regain control.

This wasn't good.

Gray, who was still out of his seat, was flung to the floor but he was too far out of reach for Hunter to make a grab for him.

They seemed to gather speed, the confused shouts in the dark adding to the sense of disorientation. The coach veered off down some sort of embankment, branches clawing at the windows failing to slow them down. Glass smashed all around as gnarly limbs reached in and grabbed at the passengers inside.

He glanced over at Charlotte, who was hanging on to the armrest so hard her knuckles were white. He hated being this helpless, pinned by his seat belt as they hurtled at speed and unable to protect her. The driver was hitting the brakes and doing his best to swerve through the trees threatening their survival.

After what seemed an eternity of pinballing between obstacles in their path, there was another loud crash. Even Hunter was lifted out of his seat with the force of the impact as the vehicle hit its final resting place, wedged into a tree trunk.

For a few stunned seconds the only sound was the dying breath of the engine and the flickering headlights before they gave up the ghost and plunged them into complete darkness. He fumbled in his pocket for his cellphone to call for help but there was no signal. At least it came in handy as a torch if nothing else. Some of the others had had the same idea and fireflies of light began to appear in the shadows. He undid his seat belt and went to Charlotte first.

'Are you okay?' He shone the light in her face, forcing her to blink. She was pale but conscious and the relief was so overwhelming it was all he could do not to gather her up into his arms and hug her tight.

'I'm fine. You?'

'I'm good.' Now he knew she wasn't badly hurt.

'Can you smell smoke?'

Hunter sniffed the air and swore. There was no mistaking that acrid odour slowly filling the bus and his lungs.

'We need to see who's been hurt.' She unclipped her seat belt, her thoughts firmly on the welfare of everyone else.

'We've got to get them as far from here as possible.' From the front of the bus he could see the smoke curling out from beneath the crumpled hood and there was no time to waste.

The electrics were shot so he was forced to use brute strength to prise the doors open and let some much-needed air into the vehicle. He helped the driver stagger outside into the night first and went back to assist those who needed it.

'Gray? Can you hear me?' Charlotte was kneeling by Gray, checking his pulse. He was lying face down in the aisle, unmoving, and blocking the exit route for everyone else.

Hunter went cold at the thought of the injuries he could've sustained, tossed around like a ragdoll. Unlike everyone else, he'd been on his feet, unsecured and unprotected, as they'd bumped and smashed their way down the embankment. While Charlotte took care of Gray, he quickly checked the bus for other casualties but luckily everyone else seemed okay.

'Guys, can you make your way out of the emergency exit at the back and get as far from the bus as you can, please?' he shouted to those moving about at the back so they weren't putting themselves in more danger by waiting here if there was a chance of fire on board.

He crouched down beside Charlotte, holding his own breath and waiting desperately to hear any sound of life coming from his friend on the floor.

There was a moan as Gray came to and let Hunter breathe again.

'We have to get him out of here.'

'We really shouldn't move him until we know the extent of his injuries. He took quite a knock back there.' The doctor in Charlotte protested about the proposed evacuation and he understood why—she didn't want to exacerbate any injuries he'd already received, but they were fast running out of options.

'Charlotte, we have to move. Now.'

She followed his gaze outside, where flames were already beginning to lick at the windscreen.

'Okay, but we need to be careful.'

'On the count of three we'll roll him over onto his back. One...'

'Two...'

'Three.'

Charlotte cradled Gray's head so he wasn't jarred too much and Hunter eased him into a better position for them to help him. He was breathing at least and there was no sign of blood. That didn't mean there weren't any internal injuries but they couldn't leave him here. Charlotte was already coughing violently and Hunter's eyes were streaming from the effects of the smoke. If they left him here he'd die from smoke inhalation alone.

'You come down this end and take his feet and I'll do the heavy lifting.' It was going to be awkward trying to get him off this bus in one piece but he knew neither of them were leaving without him.

With another count of three they managed to lift him off the floor. Charlotte backed down the aisle, steering

Hunter towards the door with Gray's full weight resting
in his arms. His lungs burned with the effort as they stumbled their way down the couple of steps. They didn't stop
even when they got outside just in case there was a fuel
leak that could see them all blown sky high.

'Careful setting him down,' Charlotte reminded him
as they reached the road, where the rest of the guys were.
A few of them bundled their jackets together to pull together a makeshift bed so at least they weren't laying him
directly on the cold, wet tarmac.

Hunter had never been as glad in his life to hear Gray
groan as they set him down and he knew his stubborn
friend would be okay.

'Is everyone else here?' Hunter yelled to the crowd
standing at the side of the road.

'We'll do a head count.' Charlotte made sure Gray was
comfortable before she was back on her feet, giving everyone a provisional check-over and singling out those she
suspected needed medical treatment. 'You have some cuts
on your face. There could be some glass left in there. Take
a seat on that tree stump over there. Has anyone phoned
for an ambulance?'

'Wait, where's Scotty?' As far as Hunter could see at
first glance the team was all here but their kit man was
noticeably absent.

'I thought he was behind us.' Floret confirmed he'd
been on the bus but there was no sign of him in this current line-up.

'I'll go back and look for him.' He wouldn't be able
to live with himself if he'd left someone behind in the
wreckage.

'Hunter, you can't.' He felt Charlotte's hand on his arm
but even her touch wasn't enough to deter him from doing
what was right. Scotty had family too and he knew if he'd

been in the same position he'd want someone looking out for him.

'I have to. I promise I'll be careful.'

'In that case, I'm coming with you.' Charlotte stubbornly strode alongside him and he knew he was wasting time fighting a losing battle.

'Scotty? Are you here?' he bellowed as they reached the clearing where the bus was barely recognisable as anything other than a cloud of smoke.

'Over there.' Charlotte pointed towards a flash of colour in the midst of the grey, a small figure sitting huddled on the ground at the back of the bus.

'Scotty? You can't stay here. The bus is on fire.' He hooked a hand under his elbow and helped him to his feet but the stunned kit man didn't seem to grasp the severity of the situation.

'Let's go.' Charlotte was there as always when he needed a hand and took Scotty's other arm so they were able to hurry him away from the scene. As they climbed the embankment towards safety there was a loud bang and the sound of smashing glass as the fire took hold and blew out what was left of the windows. It had been a close call, as his pulse rate would attest to.

'Scotty, are you all right? Talk to me.'

He heard the concern in Charlotte's voice a fraction of a second before their patient's legs went from beneath him and he collapsed, a deadweight in their arms. They had no choice but to fall to the ground with him only metres away from the road.

Charlotte felt his forehead. 'His skin is clammy.'

She took his wrist. 'His pulse is rapid and faint. I think he's going into shock.'

Hunter positioned him on the ground so his head was low and his legs were raised and supported to increase the flow of blood to his head. Charlotte loosened the collar of his shirt to make it easier for him to breathe.

The distant sound of sirens filtered through the night.

'We need to keep him warm.' Charlotte whipped her jacket from around her shoulders and tucked it in around him. 'The ambulance is on the way, Scotty. Give me a nod that you understand what's happening.'

There was a small acknowledgement.

Charlotte was working hard to keep him engaged, checking his level of response, and Hunter knew it was because there was a danger this was more than emotional shock after the accident. It could also be a life-threatening medical condition as a result of insufficient blood flow through the body, leading to a heart attack or organ damage.

'Hello?' The crunch of forest debris underfoot and sweeping torch beams dancing in the distance signalled the arrival of the emergency services, guided by a few of the players.

'We're over here!' Hunter shouted, and waved them over.

Charlotte gave the rundown of injuries, the most serious ones being Gray's and Scotty's. The paramedics ably took over, checking Scotty's vitals and wrapping him in a warm blanket. As Hunter and Charlotte got up from the damp earth, she began shivering uncontrollably. He held her close, trying to transfer some body heat.

'We should get you seen too.'

'I'll be all right. I just have to make sure the others get checked over at the hospital and I'll go back to the hotel for a bath and bed. You should probably let Alfie know we're okay in case the press gets hold of the news we've had an accident.'

'I will as soon as I know you're going to be okay.' He

was a little taken aback she was thinking about Alfie when she'd been so sure she didn't want to be part of their family. That instinct to reassure him, the knowledge his welfare was the uppermost thought in her mind, said she was already invested in them both. It was a revelation that changed his own ideas about what was best for all of them. If there was a chance they could be together and work this out, he wanted to cling to it.

'I can't believe you followed me down here.'

'I wasn't just going to sit back and watch you get hurt, now, was I?' She'd put herself at risk for him and Hunter struggled with the urge to kiss her. In that moment all that mattered was that she was safe. He brushed away bits of leaves and twigs that had become tangled in her hair along the way and the movement revealed a small cut on her forehead he'd missed up until now.

'You're hurt.' He reached out and sticky blood coated his fingers.

'I banged my head on the seat in front when we hit that tree. I'll probably have an egg-shaped reminder in the morning.' She moved her hair back over her face to hide it, as if that would somehow solve the problem.

'You could have whiplash or concussion even. You know what could happen if that's left untreated. Do you have any pain? Blurred vision?' Head injuries, especially those caused by a high-impact crash, could lead to serious complications, ones he wasn't going to risk.

'Hey, who's the doctor here? I think you've a tendency to overstep your jurisdiction, Mr Torrance.' Her defences were back up as she stepped back from him and out of his hold.

Unfortunately, it was in that second her knees buckled and belied that she wasn't as indestructible as she made out. Hunter made a grab for her before she could hit the ground and scooped her up into his arms. Despite her huge personality, she weighed virtually nothing and he was reminded of how vulnerable she really was despite her insistence otherwise. He wasn't prepared to take any risks where her health was concerned.

She might claim she didn't want him in her life but that didn't mean he'd simply stop caring about her. She'd made an impression on his heart that could never be erased, even if he did move to London.

'Let's get you into the ambulance with the others.' He carried her up through the trees himself, with no intention of leaving her until he knew she was safe.

Charlotte's head was in a whirl and it wasn't entirely down to the knock she'd taken in last night's crash. Hunter's words and actions towards her simply didn't marry. One minute she was finding out he was planning a move to London with no thought for her, the next he was refusing to leave her hospital bedside, playing the role of a concerned partner. It wasn't fair when she was supposed to be getting used to not having him around. How could she remain aloof and disinterested in someone who was so clearly passionate about helping others, and about her?

He'd stayed with her until she'd been discharged in the early hours of the morning when she'd assured the medical staff she'd return if any other symptoms of concussion occurred. Gray had been kept in for observation and apparently they'd run a battery of tests on Scotty too. When she'd begged the nurses for information they'd told her he was on an IV for fluid resuscitation to raise his blood pressure again and they were looking at an ECG and bloods to determine any underlying heart problems. A bump on the head seemed minor in comparison but Hunter had insisted she get checked over too.

He'd even offered to stay with her back at the hotel—
on the floor, of course—in case she needed him during
the night. She hadn't accepted his offer because one night
simply wasn't enough any more. She wanted for ever. For
too long she'd been denying she was in love with the man
because she'd known it would bring her nothing but heartache, and she'd been right. When she'd found out about
the job in London the sense of betrayal, the knowledge
he would happily abandon her in pursuit of his ego, had
turned her into that wounded, lonely girl again.

In the end she hadn't even had breakfast with him. He'd
been a complete no-show for the meal with the team, and
was still missing here at training. Uneasiness settled heavily in her stomach along with the few bites of toast she'd
managed. She knew where he was, he was off making great
plans for his future in London without her.

Last night had proved to her how far she'd fallen for him
because she'd never been as scared in her life as she'd been
when he'd said he was going back to that bus. She didn't
want to imagine her life without him in it if something
had happened to him. It didn't matter because she hadn't
fought any harder than he had to save the relationship and
he'd taken that as her acceptance of his choice to leave.

If she'd only told him she was in love with him, that she
wanted to spend every day with him and Alfie, he might've
stayed, but she'd been too scared to take that risk and she'd
lost him anyway. She didn't know whether to laugh or cry
at her own stupidity, continuing to let the past overshadow
the good things in her life now, and in the early hours of
the morning it had been a hideous combination of both.

There was one familiar face waiting at the arena for
practice but it wasn't the one she'd hoped to see.

'Gray? What on earth are you doing here?'

'The same as everyone else, I expect,' he said, coming to watch the drills out on the ice alongside her.

She rolled her eyes at him. 'You know very well what I mean. What are you doing out of hospital?'

'They sent me home so someone who actually needed a bed could have one.' He folded down one of the seats and gingerly sat down, clutching his right side.

'Hmm. Well, if they *actually* discharged you I'm sure they told you to rest.' She doubted his version of events. If nothing else, they were supposed to notify her when he was released to avoid this very situation.

'Nothing's broken, just a couple of badly bruised ribs.' He adjusted his position and sucked in a breath even with that minimal effort.

'I'm sure it's still painful though.' It didn't take a doctor to know that sitting all day in an uncomfortable chair in a cold arena wasn't going to help a rib injury.

He patted his jacket pocket. 'I've got my painkillers right here. It'll take more than a few bruised ribs for me to miss this game.'

'Well, take it as easy as you can.' Which was akin to asking a lion not to roar, but she was well aware nothing she said would persuade him to rest and aid healing.

'How are the rest of the guys? Are they fit enough to win?'

'They're a bit shaken up, battered and bruised, but there's nothing to rule them out of playing. Scotty got the all-clear too but he's doing the sensible thing and staying in bed, like he was told.'

It might be harder to keep their minds on the game after the shock of the crash. Although now Gray was here it would be a relief for them to see him and he'd certainly be a motivator to get them going. That only left one of their party MIA.

'Good.'

'Did, uh, Hunter pick you up from the hospital?' She was grasping for a rational, painless explanation for his absence. If Gray had discharged himself, as she suspected, he would've sworn any accomplice to secrecy until the deed was done.

'I phoned a cab. Where is he anyway?' He turned his head as much as his injury would allow to scour the building.

'He had to…er…take care of something. I said I would manage here until he got back.' The lie burned her tongue as well as her cheeks in the knowledge he hadn't trusted her with any such courtesy.

As it turned out, Hunter didn't make an appearance until training was over, and then without a hint of urgency in his swagger.

'You do know the season isn't over yet?' Gray arched an eyebrow at him, clearly not amused by his sudden unreliability.

Hunter shrugged off his jacket and rolled up his sleeves. 'I do know and I'm here with plenty of time to spare before the big game.'

'I hope so, for your sake.'

'Uh, Gray? I need to have a word with you. In private.' He flicked a glance at Charlotte, sufficient to justify her paranoia.

Only a few hours ago he hadn't wanted to leave her side. Now it appeared she was somehow in the way, a nuisance he couldn't wait to be rid of.

'Don't mind me. I'm only here to do a job after all.' She bristled past the two men before her anguish at her dismissal manifested in not very professional tears of self-pity.

When it came to Hunter choosing between her and, well, anything, she knew she'd lose every time.

'I do hope your personal problems aren't leaking into your career prospects again,' Gray said as they both watched Charlotte storm off.

There was no point in pretending he had the wrong idea about their relationship when she showed her emotions so clearly for everyone to see. Right now, they could both see she was royally ticked off at him.

'That's exactly what I'm trying to avoid and why I wanted to talk to you.' He inhaled a lungful of air to fortify himself. It wasn't going to be an easy conversation with any of those affected by his future plans.

Gray fixed him with a steely stare. 'You've been given a second chance here.'

'For which I'll be eternally in your debt. I don't want to mess things up with Alfie, that's why I've had to make a few tough decisions.'

'That doesn't sound good. You do know I'm recovering from my injuries here and my team, which has just been in a road accident, is about to play in the final? Couldn't this wait?'

Hunter understood Gray's frustration. It was bad timing, like every other major event in his life. The difference was that he was taking control this time, not simply letting events carry him along.

Work got in the way of the talk he so desperately needed to have with Charlotte. Although they'd been given the all-clear last night, a lot of the guys were suffering from more aches and pains than usual as a result of the accident. The trauma and exposure had kept him up to his elbows in deep-tissue massages for most of the morning. He was running out of time to set the record straight with her but he couldn't let the team down now. This was the last time he'd have the opportunity to show Gray he'd been worth the risk. If he got the Demons fighting fit to win this final they might forgive him for trying to walk out on them. Even if Charlotte couldn't.

They kept missing each other, with players coming and going between them, and having to grab breaks where they could. Not that this conversation was ever going to be one they could squeeze in between patients.

It wasn't until near the end of the game she ventured down into the tunnel, away from the bench and a mass audience.

'About this morning...' This wasn't the time or place he'd been hoping to have this conversation, with the soundtrack of bodies slamming into the hoardings playing in the background, but he needed to explain what had happened.

'Is it a done deal?'

'Pardon?' Her need to get straight to the point always threw him. That's why it had made her reluctance to talk through the end of their relationship so hard to come to terms with.

'Is it too late?'

'For what?'

'Us.'

It took a moment for the line of her questioning to register and when it did it felt as though a weight had been lifted off his chest. That didn't mean he was happy to be left guessing exactly what it was she wanted this time.

'What are you saying, Charlotte? It was only yesterday you were telling me there was no way this could work, that you didn't want to be part of my and Alfie's lives.' He still had to be careful that she meant this—that she knew exactly what she was getting into and didn't run out on him again when it hit home.

'I was scared, Hunter, afraid to get close in case I'm not

enough to keep you happy. Last night when I thought you might get hurt…it made me realise it doesn't matter how much I fight it, I'm already in love with you. I'm sorry I let my fears get in the way of what we had, what we could have if you'll still have me. I should've been prepared to take a risk, the way you did in letting me into your life with Alfie. Is there still a chance? Do you love me?' She barely took a breath and left Hunter dizzy with the rapid speed of her admissions, but there was only one thing that mattered at the end of all this. She loved him.

'Of course I love you!' When she'd been hurt last night it had become very clear to him how much she meant to him. He would've swapped places with her himself if he'd been able to and taken away even the slightest discomfort for her. He loved her and it was time to stop running away from the fact.

When she'd had doubts about being part of his family he'd snatched hold of that excuse and used it to justify a move to London. She was right, the first sign of trouble and his instinct was to run. Not any more. This time he was prepared to stay and fight.

Last night had made him see everything in a different light. She hadn't given a thought for her own safety in the chaos, following him back to the accident site to ensure his. Then there'd been her concern for Alfie, the boy she'd tried to convince herself and him she could never get close to. They were meant to be together, to be a family, if only they could face their fears instead of being overwhelmed by them.

She took a deep breath. 'That's all I needed to know… If London is where you're going to be, I'll come too. I'm sure I can set up my practice there just as easily. I'll do whatever it takes for us to make a real go of this. You and Alfie are worth the risk.' Her smile as she handed her heart to him

on a plate just about broke him. He'd never imagined anyone could love him enough to give up everything for him.

'You would really do that?'

'I'll go and hand my resignation in to Gray as soon as
the match is over.'

'You don't have to, Charlotte. I'm not going to London.
I met with CC this morning to tell him I'm staying put.
Everything I want is in Ireland and right here.' When he'd
sat at that desk across from his prospective new boss and
the life he'd laid out before him it had all seemed so cold
and impersonal without Charlotte in it. He'd almost had
the perfect family he'd always wanted and had been close
to throwing it all away. He'd been willing to crawl to the
ends of the earth to retrieve that final missing piece of the
puzzle. Charlotte had simply got there first. 'Perhaps I was
keeping you at a bit of a distance because I was worried
I'd hurt you the way I hurt Sara. There's one glaringly obvious difference between then and now. I never loved her
the way I love you.'

'But—but what about Gray? Have you handed in your
resignation already?'

'That's why I wanted to speak to him, for confirmation I would still have a job with the Demons next season so I know I have something to offer you other than
another dead-in-the-water career.' He'd been honest with
Gray about what had happened, risking their friendship
over the betrayal, but he was a father too and he'd understood his motives. Right before he'd told him to move his
butt and get back to work before face-off.

Goal!

As they turned to face each other and confront the situation, the celebrations around the arena stalled the response
he'd been waiting to hear all day. They were so locked in
that moment, intent on finally resolving their status, nei-

ther even turned to see who'd scored. Although they did share a smile when the announcement came that Anderson had put the Demons ahead.

'I guess our jobs are safe for another season, huh?' He cracked a joke because he was afraid those three words he'd waited a lifetime to say had come too late. This wasn't Hollywood, there was no guarantee they'd just run titles and walk off into the sunset because he'd broken out the 'I love you' speech.

Charlotte was stunned by the news that he'd given up a new job and a move to London all for her. 'You really mean it?'

'I really mean it.'

He grabbed her hand and placed it on his chest. A definite ploy to stop her from thinking straight when that solid muscle beneath her fingers brought back memories of their night together, exploring each other's bodies until she'd known every inch of him.

'Do you feel that? My heart is pumping with adrenaline, waiting for you to tell me that you want to be with me and Alfie.'

'You were, are, the best thing to ever happen to me. I didn't know what living was until you two came along.'

She could tell how much he'd struggled, trying to combine parenthood with everything else. The worry lines were etched deeply on his brow and she dared to move closer to test the theory this wasn't the same man who'd planned to run away from her when the going got tough.

'I love you, Charlotte. I still want that fresh start but this time I want it with you. No secrets, no pretending I know what's best for everyone else, just open and honest discussion about what we want, or where we go, as a family.'

'A family?' She needed someone to pinch her and prove this was real, not a dream conjured up by her broken heart.

'You. Me. Alfie. Together. For ever.'

'I couldn't think of anything more perfect.' She wound her arms around his neck and snuggled in close, willing to risk everything she had for a chance of happiness.

Somewhere far away the final klaxon sounded and declared the Demons play-off champions, but it was Charlotte who felt like the real winner now they'd both shaken off the shadows of the past for a future together.

EPILOGUE

'HOW DID IT GO?' Charlotte hadn't been able to settle all afternoon, waiting to hear how Hunter's meeting had gone with Alfie's teacher.

It had been a whirlwind of a year for all of them and she hoped it hadn't affected his schoolwork. There'd been the move into the cottage and getting used to living together as a family and the rushed wedding when they'd decided life was too short to waste any more time. It was a lot for a young boy to deal with all at once.

And her.

That parental guilt she'd worried about all along had well and truly kicked in but she wouldn't be without either of them for the world.

Hunter sat on the end of her desk. 'It went great. Mrs Patterson said he's top of the class for reading and maths.'

She could stop sweating now she'd been reassured his new stepmother wasn't responsible for a decline in his grades. He didn't appear unhappy with the new arrangement, he was as good as gold for her. She simply worried constantly about his well-being. It was taking a lot of willpower not to become a helicopter parent. Especially when she might be in danger of upsetting the family dynamic again.

'I'm so glad. He's been through a lot.'

'To quote his favourite teacher, "He's a happy, well-adjusted little boy."'

Hearing that made her well up because it was so important to her. Plus she was a tad hormonal these days.

'I'm sorry I couldn't make it in time. My appointment overran, otherwise I would've been there too.'

'I know, sweetheart. It's fine. You were there for his school play when I couldn't make it. That's part of the reason we make such a good team. There will always be at least one of us there waving pom-poms for him.'

It was true, they were a great team in all aspects of their lives. Gray had been only too happy to sign them both on for the new season and when the office next door to hers came onto the market Hunter had been able to set his own private practice up too. They shared the parenting as much as they could, with a little help from the O'Reillys every now and then.

'Where is he?'

'With his grandparents. They suggested we might like to go out to dinner or something while they babysit tonight.'

'Or something?' She hadn't missed the fact he'd locked the door on his way in. A clear indication they wouldn't make it out in time for dinner.

His cheeky grin said he had more than food on his mind too. 'Are you finished here?'

'For now. I need to write up a few progress reports for Gray but I can do that before the next match.'

'I can't believe it's play-off season already. That means a certain one-year anniversary. Perhaps we should celebrate?' He waggled his eyebrows. As if she needed reminding what they'd got up to this time last year. They'd done a lot more since.

'We can celebrate but it'll have to be minus the alcohol.' The news she'd been hiding was bubbling to the surface.

'You're not feeling sick again, are you?' He reached out to feel her forehead.

'I have a confession to make. I had an appointment today but as a patient, not a doctor.'

'You're scaring me now. Why didn't you tell me there was something wrong?' He scrambled off the desk and took her hand, his concern touching.

'I wanted to confirm my own diagnosis first. I think we're on our way to starting our own little hockey team.' She moved his hand to her belly, which was apparently full of more than Hunter's maple syrup pancakes.

'You're pregnant?' His eyes were like saucers as his slack jaw gradually widened into the happiest, sexiest smile she'd ever seen. She hadn't known men could get the pregnancy bloom too but he was beaming from the inside out.

'*We're* pregnant. I expect you to be with me in this every step of the way.' As happy as she was at the news too, there was a little trepidation at what the next few months had in store.

'Don't worry, there's nowhere I'd rather be than right here.' He placed a soft kiss on her belly to confirm they were in this together.

This baby was a new beginning for all of them. One they all deserved.

* * * * *

*If you enjoyed this story, check out these
other great reads from Karin Baine*

FALLING FOR THE FOSTER MUM
THE COURAGE TO LOVE HER ARMY DOC
THE DOCTOR'S FORBIDDEN FLING
A KISS TO CHANGE HER LIFE

All available now!

MILLS & BOON®
Hardback – July 2017

ROMANCE

MILLS & BOON®
Large Print – July 2017

ROMANCE

Secrets of a Billionaire's Mistress	Sharon Kendrick
Claimed for the De Carrillo Twins	Abby Green
The Innocent's Secret Baby	Carol Marinelli
The Temporary Mrs Marchetti	Melanie Milburne
A Debt Paid in the Marriage Bed	Jennifer Hayward
The Sicilian's Defiant Virgin	Susan Stephens
Pursued by the Desert Prince	Dani Collins
Return of Her Italian Duke	Rebecca Winters
The Millionaire's Royal Rescue	Jennifer Faye
Proposal for the Wedding Planner	Sophie Pembroke
A Bride for the Brooding Boss	Bella Bucannon

HISTORICAL

Surrender to the Marquess	Louise Allen
Heiress on the Run	Laura Martin
Convenient Proposal to the Lady	Julia Justiss
Waltzing with the Earl	Catherine Tinley
At the Warrior's Mercy	Denise Lynn

MEDICAL

Falling for Her Wounded Hero	Marion Lennox
The Surgeon's Baby Surprise	Charlotte Hawkes
Santiago's Convenient Fiancée	Annie O'Neil
Alejandro's Sexy Secret	Amy Ruttan
The Doctor's Diamond Proposal	Annie Claydon
Weekend with the Best Man	Leah Martyn

MILLS & BOON®
Hardback – August 2017

ROMANCE

An Heir Made in the Marriage Bed	Anne Mather
The Prince's Stolen Virgin	Maisey Yates
Protecting His Defiant Innocent	Michelle Smart
Pregnant at Acosta's Demand	Maya Blake
The Secret He Must Claim	Chantelle Shaw
Carrying the Spaniard's Child	Jennie Lucas
A Ring for the Greek's Baby	Melanie Milburne
Bought for the Billionaire's Revenge	Clare Connelly
The Runaway Bride and the Billionaire	Kate Hardy
The Boss's Fake Fiancée	Susan Meier
The Millionaire's Redemption	Therese Beharrie
Captivated by the Enigmatic Tycoon	Bella Bucannon
Tempted by the Bridesmaid	Annie O'Neil
Claiming His Pregnant Princess	Annie O'Neil
A Miracle for the Baby Doctor	Meredith Webber
Stolen Kisses with Her Boss	Susan Carlisle
Encounter with a Commanding Officer	Charlotte Hawkes
Rebel Doc on Her Doorstep	Lucy Ryder
The CEO's Nanny Affair	Joss Wood
Tempted by the Wrong Twin	Rachel Bailey

MILLS & BOON®
Large Print – August 2017

ROMANCE

The Italian's One-Night Baby	Lynne Graham
The Desert King's Captive Bride	Annie West
Once a Moretti Wife	Michelle Smart
The Boss's Nine-Month Negotiation	Maya Blake
The Secret Heir of Alazar	Kate Hewitt
Crowned for the Drakon Legacy	Tara Pammi
His Mistress with Two Secrets	Dani Collins
Stranded with the Secret Billionaire	Marion Lennox
Reunited by a Baby Bombshell	Barbara Hannay
The Spanish Tycoon's Takeover	Michelle Douglas
Miss Prim and the Maverick Millionaire	Nina Singh

HISTORICAL

Claiming His Desert Princess	Marguerite Kaye
Bound by Their Secret Passion	Diane Gaston
The Wallflower Duchess	Liz Tyner
Captive of the Viking	Juliet Landon
The Spaniard's Innocent Maiden	Greta Gilbert

MEDICAL

Their Meant-to-Be Baby	Caroline Anderson
A Mummy for His Baby	Molly Evans
Rafael's One Night Bombshell	Tina Beckett
Dante's Shock Proposal	Amalie Berlin
A Forever Family for the Army Doc	Meredith Webber
The Nurse and the Single Dad	Dianne Drake

MILLS & BOON®

Why shop at millsandboon.co.uk?

Each year, thousands of romance readers find their
perfect read at millsandboon.co.uk. That's because
we're passionate about bringing you the very best
romantic fiction. Here are some of the advantages
of shopping at www.millsandboon.co.uk:

* **Get new books first**—you'll be able to buy your
  favourite books one month before they hit
  the shops

* **Get exclusive discounts**—you'll also be able to buy
  our specially created monthly collections, with up
  to 50% off the RRP

* **Find your favourite authors**—latest news,
  interviews and new releases for all your favourite
  authors and series on our website, plus ideas for
  what to try next

* **Join in**—once you've bought your favourite books,
  don't forget to register with us to rate, review and
  join in the discussions

Visit **www.millsandboon.co.uk**
for all this and more today!